MARIAH'S MARRIAGE

1822: Scholarly Mariah Fox is fiercely dedicated to her work of educating London urchins. When she is charged by a stray pig, and quite literally falls into the arms of Tobias Longreach, her life changes forever . . . For Tobias, the Earl of Mellon, requires a wife to provide an heir — and decides that Mariah will do very nicely. But the sinister Sir Lucas Wellwood, burdened by debt, has been urging his sister Araminta to secure Tobias's hand for herself— and will stop at nothing to get his hands on the earl's wealth . . .

ANNE STENHOUSE

MARIAH'S MARRIAGE

Complete and Unabridged

LINFORD
Leicester

First published in Great Britain in 2013

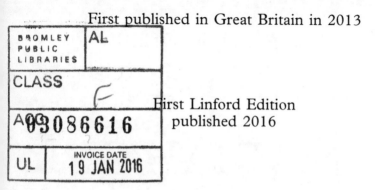

First Linford Edition
published 2016

Copyright © 2013 by Anne Stenhouse

A catalogue record for this book is available
from the British Library.

ISBN 978–1–4448–2732–3

Published by
F. A. Thorpe (Publishing)
Anstey, Leicestershire

Set by Words & Graphics Ltd.
Anstey, Leicestershire
Printed and bound in Great Britain by
T. J. International Ltd., Padstow, Cornwall

This book is printed on acid-free paper

1

London, 1822

Mariah Fox stabbed a long pin through her straw bonnet, attaching it to her upswept mass of ash-blonde hair. She tied the ribbons beneath her chin, drew back capable shoulders, and stepped into the street. The city air, heavy with the rank smell of the Thames and the fumes of a nearby tanner's yard, struck her in the face.

She'd spent an hour teaching sixty urchins their letters, and their unwashed state was only just preferable to the smells on the street. Nonetheless, the class was the high point of Mariah's week, and today one of the boys had recited his letters all the way through.

'Watch yer feet there, missy!' a youth shouted as he hefted a load of rags newly-tumbled off his mate's barrow.

'Too dainty they are ter get into any 'orse muck.'

Mariah pulled back, just in time to avoid a steaming mound of horse droppings, and sent a grateful smile towards the lad. She pushed her fingers into the pocket of her pelisse and found a coin to spin in his direction.

'You shouldn't have done that, Mariah,' Peter Sharp, her companion, said. 'He'll only spend it on ale.'

'I think he earned it, Peter. He may spend it as he chooses,' Mariah replied and wished again that her papa had less faith in this sallow-complexioned man, now in middle-age. He seemed to make it his business to drive joy from the air. 'Besides, I have to clean my own boots at present, so I am grateful,' she added.

'The latest boy has proved no better than any of the others your papa takes on?' Peter asked, and Mariah hated the smug smile that tugged around the corners of his mouth. How she wished she could say the boy was excellent beyond expectation.

'Alas, no. He ran off two nights ago with a flagon of cider and a side of ham. Cook is very cross.'

'It passes my understanding how a man of such superior intellect can be constantly duped.'

And mine, Mariah thought, since he trusts you with the care of my classes. Peter's sanctimonious views irritated Mariah afresh. She increased her step and left the safety of the pavement without sufficient attention. A loose pig charged towards them and she backed away instinctively, catching her foot against the kerbstone and falling into the arms of a passing stranger.

'I say, sir,' Peter began, but his blustering was quelled into silence.

Mariah was dimly aware of him holding back while the stranger lifted her from danger. The strength flowing from her rescuer calmed her nerves, and she lay against his chest for a long moment. It was not until she realised he was struggling to keep laughter at bay that she wriggled to be free.

'My escort is right, sir,' she protested. 'While I thank you for rescuing me from an inglorious bump, I am quite able to stand.'

'I regret that very much,' the stranger said, and his voice held warmth Mariah was sure must draw others to him. 'However, I cannot allow my baser instincts to take advantage over such a fortuitous meeting.' He repositioned her on the flagstones, keeping hold of her elbow for a moment or two.

Mariah straightened her bonnet and brushed down her clothes while she regained a little self-possession. The stranger was not as young as she might have thought at first, probably around thirty years of age. He had good colour, indicating he spent much time out-of-doors, and he carried himself with an air that told Mariah he was used to command. She suspected he might be an army officer or half-pay captain.

'Out of harm's way, ma'am,' the stranger said, and she recognised the accent of her late mama's county,

Somerset. 'The streets are very busy at this time in the day. Why, I was nearly bowled over myself two minutes ago by a troop of urchins fleeing from this very building.'

'That was the class Miss Fox was teaching, sir,' Peter said. 'If one of them attacked you, then you must say what he was like and he shall feel the weight of my cane next week.'

'I cannot think he will remember from one week to the next,' Mariah protested.

'Much as their attitude to learning their letters, then,' Peter said, and Mariah closed her eyes lest he see the annoyance there. When would Papa realise what an inhibition Peter Sharp was to their prospects of teaching any child his letters?

'I think the young lady probably uses different methods to achieve her ends; and besides,' the man said, with a smile in his voice that matched the twinkle in his brown eyes, 'it was ever the case that the young male would escape as quickly as possible from confinement in a classroom. Even when the lessons were presided over with such grace.' He bowed.

Mariah felt a warm blush stain her cheeks. This man was flirting with her. How had she allowed herself to become an object of gallantry?

'Peter, I think Papa will wonder why we are late,' she said; and, with a swift nod in the direction of her tormentor, turned away.

'A moment, ma'am.' The man briefly touched his gloved hand to her elbow. 'I would send you home in my carriage, but I have urgent business that cannot be delayed. Let me call a hackney.' He turned to face the busy street, and within seconds a horse and carriage drew out from the press of carts and barrows to pull up beside them.

'This is not necessary, sir,' Mariah protested. 'I am used to walking, and fit.'

'I do not doubt, but you are trembling and I think your constitution may have sustained more of a shock than you believe,' he said as he hauled open the door of the carriage and brought down the step. 'Humour me.' He took her hand to guide her up into the vehicle.

Peter hesitated and then followed, calling out, 'Redde Place,' to the driver. 'Stop at the house with the blue doors.'

Her unnamed rescuer passed some coins to the driver and stood back to allow the carriage to pull away. Mariah caught the satisfied expression his features settled into, and knew full well his explanation was all flummery.

'How easily he referred to my constitution when in reality he can know nothing about me,' she said crossly. 'Did he make up all that nonsense so that he could hear my address?'

'I suppose you think I supplied it too easily, Mariah, but I wanted to get you out of his way as quickly as possible.'

She smiled a little at Peter's pettish

tone. It was exactly what she did think, but she knew from past occasions not to let him work himself up over a supposed criticism. He would embroider the incident out of all recognition and cause her papa discomfort when the gentleman had simply been amusing himself.

'Do not distress yourself, Peter, please. I do not mean to criticise and we are not used to games of concealment. It is most likely we will never see the gentleman again. We do not even know his name.'

'I trust that is not a matter of regret to you. He is not the sort of man I would wish you to associate with.' Peter used his most severe schoolmaster's voice.

'I cannot think why you believe I regret not learning his name or having any prospect of seeing him again, but it need not concern you, Peter. Should he present himself at Redde Place, Papa will send him about his business,' Mariah said a little more sharply than she had intended. Why did Peter think he was entitled to an opinion on whom might be included in her circle of acquaintance?

'We must not dismiss the possibility that the gentleman is progressive,' she added mischievously, 'and would welcome an introduction to a reliable teacher for any workers he may have.'

Peter did not reply but squared his shoulders in a way which was becoming more familiar to Mariah than she wanted. How she wished her papa would allow their maid Tilly to escort her when she next went to teach the urchins. Tilly with a broom in her hands would tame even the most unruly of fellows. She supposed it would not do for two such young women to be alone with sixty ill-disciplined wretches. Perhaps she would have to put up with Peter's company if she wanted to continue teaching this particular class.

★   ★   ★

As the carriage pulled into the stream of traffic, Tobias Longreach, seventh Earl of Mellon, took a deep breath. He straightened his hat and brushed some mud, left by Miss Fox's feet, from the front of his pantaloons.

'What ho, Tobias!' John Brent bellowed as he surged across the pavement from the rather dubious premises he had been visiting. Tobias knew it was the home of a money-lender. 'Good of you to come with me. I can't say I enjoy being in this part of town without a friend or two to back me up. Who was the young lady you were handing into a carriage there? Didn't seem flighty enough for an opera dancer.'

'She is a teacher, John, and far from being an opera dancer. She was escorted by an older male, I would think of her papa's choice, but perhaps an official from whatever society funds the classes.'

'The harder they fall, then, eh old boy?' John said loudly, clapping Tobias between the shoulder blades. 'A challenge for you to prise her away from her intended.'

'Intended?' Tobias repeated slowly, and a pain surged through his chest. 'Surely not? I cannot imagine any young lady with such bright blue eyes and lively smile would be intending to marry that pompous bully. It is more likely he is a long-standing friend of her papa's, or perhaps an uncle or a cousin.'

John stepped sideways at such vehemence and took out his pocket handkerchief to wave in front of Tobias. 'Come, come, Toby, my lad. Where is the characteristic Mellon coolness in the face of adversity? I know your mama is desperate for you to become leg-shackled, but she cannot have in mind a drab little teacher who works among tanners' brats.'

'No, she does not have anyone in mind apart from the entire crop of beauties being paraded at Almack's for their first, second or, in some desperate cases, third Season,' Tobias said with just a touch of asperity. 'My father did not marry her until he was well into his fortieth year, and yet she hounds me virtually every day.'

'Truth to tell, Tobias, some of your friends would be glad enough to set up home if their circumstances permitted it,' John muttered darkly, and Tobias was brought back to the reason for their visit to the area. John had had a win at the tables last night, but needed most of the blunt to repay a loan. He mentally kicked himself, but knew his friend would not appreciate overmuch sympathy for his plight.

'Things will come about for you, man,' he said with quiet sincerity. 'Your godfather cannot be immortal and he is now eighty-four,' he added, referring to the aged man who had made John his heir.

'Aye, and his father was ninety-two when he popped off. I might also be into my fifth decade before I can offer a young lady the prospect of a roof over her head. I expect you're glad the coach was hidden down a side-street,' John replied as the Mellons' town coach pulled up beside them. 'Teacher ladies would be impressed by the family crest.'

'Yes, they would. The ones searching out a husband or even a protector would be encouraged; but the genuine ones, with a calling to do good, would be discouraged.'

'Too deep for me.' John climbed into the coach. 'There's enough of my winnings left to treat you to a luncheon at my club.'

'Thanks, John, but I think I will return to Grosvenor Square and join Mama and Daisy. I know Daisy struggles to keep Mama's spirits up, even with her companion's help, and I feel I must do a little to support them.'

Tobias pondered how much to reveal to John of his mama's problems. It was known to a few that Constanzia had been prevented from making any return visits to Spain by the war in the Peninsula. What was not spread abroad was the effect his brother's death had had on her sensibilities. Tobias searched his dear friend's face and decided he must confide in someone.

'John, my mama is ill,' he said.

'I'm sorry to hear that, Toby. Is this why she wishes to travel to Spain? To make a — ' He coughed, but found the courage to go on. ' — a final visit?'

'No, it is an illness of the soul, I think. She is robust in her person, but she aches for the smells and the language, the food and the wine of her native country. It is wearing her out and I fear for her. I think she may be on the verge of an apoplexy,' Tobias concluded.

'And you do not think to have her admitted to a . . . '

'No female relative of mine will ever be incarcerated in the Bedlam or any similar hospital,' Tobias said vehemently, and he saw his friend experience some embarrassment. 'I beg your pardon, John, but I do believe these places are responsible for more

14

harm than good.'

'You could be right, man, of course you could. I would not like to see my own sisters there either,' John agreed. He ran a finger around the inside of his neck-cloth. 'But why doesn't she just take ship? You surely don't lack the funds?'

Tobias groaned. Why indeed? 'She will not go until she has resolved the issue of a wife for the heir,' he said. 'With Leo's death so soon following Papa's, she has become a little superstitious about leaving her menfolk unattended.'

John was quiet for a moment or two, and Tobias knew he would be trying to reconcile the circumstances of Leo's death to the revelation he had just made about his mama's health. He might again try to persuade him to tell her the whole, and Tobias felt weary at the prospect.

'In short, sir, you must marry,' John conceded, 'and 'tis devilish difficult while all the Society mamas are nervous about you.'

'As you say. In the meantime there are unused funds of my grandmother's, which she wished to be awarded to educational purposes. I may return here next week in order to assess whether Miss Fox's class would benefit from endowment.' When Tobias spoke the lady's name, a vision of sparkling eyes that gave promise of mischief, and perhaps a wish for excitement, flashed through his brain. He suspected she might not be as much of the education-alist stamp as her escort and her papa believed. But what was that to him?

He gazed out of the window to see an acquaintance, Sir Lucas Wellwood, and his sister Amarinta, walking along. As he watched, a group of youngsters hurtled into them just as Miss Fox's class had bowled into him earlier. Wellwood cuffed one of the boys around the head and tripped another over his outstretched walking cane before lifting it to whack the child about the shoulders.

Following his friend's gaze, John took

in the scene. 'Wellwood will injure that boy.'

Before they could intervene, a carter stepped forward and placed himself between the baronet and his victim. The man's broad frame, used to throwing around heavy loads and shoving laden carts, stopped Wellwood's arm and forced him to leave off. The little scene broke up and Wellwood turned back to his sister, who was fainting at his side.

'It's not my place to stop your carriage, of course,' John said, causing Tobias to turn towards him, 'but should we take up Miss Wellwood?'

Tobias moved his head slowly from side to side, and with one quick movement brought down the blind over the window.

'I have no time for Wellwood. Not quite a gentleman, if you know what I mean,' John persisted. 'But Miss Wellwood?'

'I find I must make haste to be back at Grosvenor Square. Sir Lucas, being her brother, is surely the best person to rescue Amarinta Wellwood.' Tobias's inner eye was filled with the picture of a laughing girl, sent off her feet but wriggling in his arms so she could be on them again as soon as may be. Miss Fox seemed to be a girl who knew how to look out for herself and to deal with emergencies.

Amarinta Wellwood was currently his mama's favourite choice in her search for a bride for her son. Orphaned into her brother's care, she did not have a society mama making difficulties about Leo's death. It was well known that Lucas expected Amarinta to marry into wealth and the peerage. Tobias could not quite like the girl, however, despite her eminent suitability. Or he could not quite like the idea of associating himself so nearly with Lucas Wellwood.

'Can an earl find his life's partner outside the charmed circle?' John asked.

Tobias closed down his expression. Perhaps his autocratic grandmother lived on in the present generation, because he found he did not like to have his actions questioned.

'I am proposing to make Miss Fox's educational project an endowment, not to consider her as a potential wife.' He instantly regretted snapping at John. Was his brain playing tricks on him? 'If you want to see Daisy, then maybe you'd like to lunch in Grosvenor Square,' he said to make amends. He saw that John was unable to prevent a slow blush covering his face when his sister was mentioned.

'That's generous of you, Toby, but I'd rather not.'

'Surely you're not put off by Daisy's lack of attention?' Tobias knew the teasing relationship between his oldest friend and his sister had cooled off recently. Perhaps, he thought, they had quarrelled over something. 'The chit thinks she's in love with some Spaniard, a relative Mama invited to visit last spring. He's too old and far too serious for her — as she would realise if she saw him again.'

'Which she will when your mama takes her to Spain after your marriage,' John said. 'She has said she is prepared to marry for duty to the family, if she cannot marry for love.'

Tobias was struck by the quiet desperation in his friend's voice. Was Daisy playing games with Brent's sensibilities? 'She's a minx, I'm afraid, John. Not that that is very different from the behaviour of many young ladies at her stage in life.' He shuddered. 'God help any man who got Daisy out of duty.' Tobias took his friend's noncommittal grunt as the closing of this topic, and leant into the cushions of his town coach.

Yes, he thought, I will go to watch Miss Fox teach. A little diversion amidst this wife-seeking will be good for me.

* * *

In Redde Place, Mariah and Peter found Mr Jerome Fox asleep over a

20

book of essays he had purchased only yesterday from Hatchard's bookshop in Picadilly. Peter coughed noisily and Jerome lifted his head. He marked his place with a letter lifted for the purpose from his cluttered desk.

'Good afternoon, Jerome. We were delayed by an unfortunate incident which occurred as we left the Chapel building,' Peter said, and Mariah sensed the dark colour wash he was going to apply to their meeting with the unnamed gentleman.

'An unfortunate incident?' Jerome's eyes raked his daughter's face. Mariah knew he was looking for any sign of distress and she smiled reassuringly at her papa. His eyes were faded in their colour now, but she remembered when they had been as blue as her own, and they were still full of intelligence as they peered out from a nest of laughter-created wrinkles. Jerome Fox might be an educationalist of standing among his peers but he was also a father of fun and good humour. 'I cannot see any lasting effect on Mariah's person, Peter, so I may conclude you met with someone not quite to your exacting standards.'

'I hope my standards are exacting, Jerome, particularly when I have your daughter in my care,' Peter said with a touch of huffiness, and Mariah suppressed another sigh. Prolonged exposure to Peter was turning her into a miss of die-away habits. She moved to take off her bonnet and pull the bell-rope for Tilly to collect it.

'Peter, will you take a little luncheon with us?' She hoped to deflect his purpose before it got underway.

'Thank you, Mariah, but Jerome may feel he needs to forego food at this time in favour of making more workable plans for your classes,' Peter said, and Mariah realised he'd felt even more sidelined by the handsome, command-ing stranger than she thought.

'I thought the class went very well. It has been a good arrangement to have milk and bread available for the boys. I recognised many of them from last week and several from the week before that,' she said calmly.

'Indeed, bribing their attendance with food produces a goodly number of learners,' Peter conceded, 'but it does not much improve their behaviour, and that is one matter I wish to bring to your attention, Jerome.'

When Mariah would have protested about the behaviour of her boys, Peter held up a hand for silence.

'Secondly, your daughter was insulted by a young buck out trawling the area for unknown purposes.' Peter screwed his mouth into a ludicrous expression of distaste and fixed his pale grey gaze on her face. Mariah returned it with poorly concealed irritation.

'Their behaviour was no worse than one would expect from children who have so little experience of sitting still, and whose hunger is not lessened much by a drink of milk and a scrap of bread.' Mariah caught sight of Tilly hovering inside the door and held her bonnet out

23

to the girl. 'I do not see how it affected the behaviour of the gentleman in any way.'

'No?' Peter exclaimed. 'Why, Mariah, he could see that a young woman whose class erupted into the street was lacking in the stern stuff needed to be out in the world on her own.'

'Mariah wasn't on her own, Peter,' Jerome said gently. 'You were with her.'

'I was. Indeed I was, but he acted as if I were invisible,' Peter said and scowled at Tilly as if she had better not listen to his next pronouncement. 'He lifted her into his arms before setting her back on the pavement.'

Mariah took pity on her papa's confusion. 'I stepped back from a charging pig, Papa, you know how they breed and run wild. I tripped over the kerbstone. The gentleman caught me before I had any chance to bang my head.'

'But to lift you into his arms . . . ' Jerome said faintly. He looked from one to the other, clearly much puzzled.

24

'I think it was probably the best way for him to catch my weight and not be knocked over.'

'Or perhaps it was an excuse to put his hands on her person,' Peter muttered darkly. 'Had he been accompanied by any friends of like mind then I do not know what might have happened to our beloved Mariah.'

Mariah straightened. How dare he imply she was his beloved? Fury left her speechless but she caught a quizzical gleam in her father's eye.

'Well, then,' Jerome said. 'Tilly, I think your mistress was about to ask if Cook has some soup ready for our midday meal. I am sure you cannot wish to devote any more of your time to us, Peter, and I will wish you good-day. We may meet this evening when Mr Bullington delivers his talk on the nature of transport without horses.'

Peter opened his mouth to speak, but must have thought better of it, and followed Tilly from the room. Jerome waited until he heard the outer door close and Tilly's feet pattering toward the back premises before he spoke again.

'Mariah, my dear child,' he said, and her spirits fell a little more. It was always the start of some horrible misapprehension on Jerome's part when he said 'my dear child'. 'Why have you not told me that an understanding exists between you and Peter?'

'Surely, Papa, you do not think I would consider an offer from Peter Sharp?'

Her father stretched out a hand, and she crossed the room to slide onto the floor at his feet. She leaned her head with its shining cap of pale curls on his lap, and he absently drew his fingers through the strands.

'I am conscious that you meet very few eligible young men. No doubt if your mama had survived she would be attending to that.'

'Papa, I am scarcely twenty-one,' Mariah said, hoping to distract her parent from his train of thought. There were so many obstacles between a married woman and any kind of meaningful industry that she did not intend to pursue marriage for several years. It was to no avail. Jerome clearly found himself wanting in his parental duties.

'However, she is not alive, and I have noticed Peter has been remarkably attentive to you since he arrived here from Manchester,' Jerome said.

'He would curtail all my freedoms and take over my classes, ruining the good work I have accomplished,' Mariah said vehemently. 'And he is not a *young* man,' she added, seeing in her mind's eye one who definitely was. A man whose muscles were etched through the cloth of his pantaloons and whose eyes sparkled with life.

'How can you say he would interfere with your work, Mariah, when he teaches mechanics himself five days a week and yet makes time to accompany you into the yards? He is a dedicated proponent of education for all.'

'He would make education a thing of fear with retributions and no rewards,' Mariah protested. 'He tried to ingratiate himself with the gentleman this afternoon by offering to cane the child who had barged into him earlier. It could not be borne.'

'Then do you intend to follow the same path as Aunt Augusta?' Jerome asked.

'Aunt Augusta? But she is married, Papa,' Mariah said.

'She did marry, my dear, but she is not *a married woman*,' Jerome said, and Mariah was astonished to see a flush of colour stain his cheeks. 'Your aunt agreed to marry in name only and has never shared a bed with Arthur Wilson. She simply wanted to put an end to our mama's constant and persistent efforts to find her a husband. They involved a great deal of socialising that took her away from her reading schedule, you see.'

Mariah struggled to her feet and

looked at her papa in confusion. 'I did not know any of this,' she said at last. 'No, Papa, I would consider such a way of life to be dishonest, I think. If I agreed to marry anyone, I would wish to be wholly their wife, although I would hope to continue with my teaching. I had thought that was how Aunt Augusta organised her life. She has always been my example.'

'We have been wont to encourage you to carry forward the fight for universal education, my dear, but I do not wish to see you unhappy in any way. If Peter gave his word that you could carry on with your teaching . . . ' Perhaps Jerome saw something in her face, because he allowed the words to trail away.

2

Exactly a week later, Mariah stood at the front of her class once more. She had dressed with more care than usual, in a round gown of pale-blue cotton that had been new last season and was very flattering to her complexion. Tilly had suggested she add a fichu of old lace around the neckline and Mariah agreed with little protest. The ripple of ivory softened her appearance more than she could have foreseen.

'Are you going on somewhere after the class, Mariah?' Peter asked as his pale gaze betrayed momentary appreciation before he shuttered it. 'That dress will get ruinously dirty.'

Of course, it was necessary to cover the whole with a sturdy apron, because the boys showed little care as yet and she was likely to be splashed with milk. *Or showered with chalk dust*, she reflected, as she wiped down the board ready for this week's lesson.

'Now, boys, who can tell me the letters known as vowels?' she asked, and watched the group for the merest hint of a hand ready to lift into the air. How she wished Peter's looming presence was elsewhere, because she was certain it held so many of them back. No matter that she would never permit its use, he insisted on carrying a stout cane with him.

In the middle of the ragged group, a tousle-headed child lifted an arm. Mariah saw the thin bones below the sleeve as it fell back and suppressed a shudder. She must see whether the ladies of this chapel could be persuaded to make broth as well as milk and bread available.

'Yes,' she said and smiled encouragement, 'can you tell me the vowels?'

'I thinks they be *a,e,u*, Miss,' the child said before subsiding into an embarrassed huddle of shyness.

Mariah wrote the three letters offered

onto her board and left a large space where she hoped the children might fill in the missing ones. There was a noise at the door and she wondered if another urchin was lurking there, too scared to enter. Out of the corner of her eye she saw Peter stiffen.

'That's a very good start, thank you. Does anyone else know a vowel?' Mariah asked calmly. No doubt the source of Peter's irritation would make itself known soon enough.

At the back of the room another boy threw his hand into the air and jumped up as Mariah pointed to him. 'I needs to go out to the privy, Miss,' he shouted, and the class laughed.

'Very well,' Mariah said and waited while the child left the room. He had done the same thing last week once he'd finished his milk, and not returned. 'Now, class, two more letters known as vowels.'

'I think they be *o* and *i*, Miss,' a large boy said.

'Who asked you to shout out of

turn?' Peter said, and Mariah stared at him in confusion. He had never actively interfered with her teaching before. What could have provoked him?

'Thank you, Mr Sharp, I am glad to hear useful suggestions even if a hand should have been raised first.' She smiled at the supposed culprit and quickly wrote 'o' and 'i' onto the board. 'Does any clever boy know of another letter that can sometimes be used as a vowel?'

'Be it y, Miss?' the same boy asked, drawing her attention back. He smiled a little in return to Mariah's warmth, but was soon cowering when Peter left his chair and stalked between the rows of benches.

'I have already told you, child, that Miss Fox may only be addressed once she has selected you after you have raised a hand. Stay behind at the end and I will impress a lesson in good manners with the cane,' Peter said. He stalked back to the front and Mariah challenged him in a whispered undertone of cold fury.

'The menace in your tone makes me think you address a known murderer, and not a ragged child so gaunt he probably hasn't eaten for a day or two.'

'Allow me to be the judge here, Mariah, unless you want these boys spinning out of control into our fine friend again,' Peter retorted, making no attempt to keep his voice down.

Indeed, she wondered if he meant his words to be overheard, and turned to look at the doorway. It was empty, but there were sounds of a minor scuffle in the passage.

Mariah drew herself up to her full height. Peter was insupportable and her papa would have to find another chaperone for her. She took a moment or two to collect her thoughts before replying.

'I am aware that discipline is needed lest the class cannot function, but bullying and brutality have no place in my teaching.' She felt the heat of her anger inflame her cheeks but would not drop her gaze from Peter's.

'I found this young man loitering around the entrance to the back court, Miss Fox,' a cultured voice said from the doorway. 'I suppose he might be one of yours.'

Mariah and Peter turned as one to the unlikely spectacle of a gentleman holding her escaped pupil by the hems of his torn jacket. The boy squirmed out of his grasp and shot into a seat near the back.

It was the gentleman who had rescued her from the pig, and she knew instantly why she had chosen the pale-blue gown and agreed to embellish it as Tilly suggested. The realisation chastened her and she could not immediately address her visitor.

'I hope I may observe the class without interfering?' the man asked. Still Mariah was at a loss. She was a teacher. She had no business dressing with the idea of impressing any male with her attractiveness. Now, if she had wanted to impress his female relatives with her suitability for the advancement of funds, she would be less confounded.

'As you see, sir,' Peter said, taking advantage of Mariah's silence, 'Miss Fox is having difficulty keeping these vagabonds under control. You bring one back from outside and I have just passed sentence on that great oaf there who talks out of turn, failing to raise his hand, which is a simple enough instruction.'

'The class seems remarkably quiet to me in comparison with my own experience at Eton College,' the gentleman said, and Mariah watched him glance around the room. She saw his eyes narrow briefly when they lighted on the 'great oaf' singled out by Peter Sharp as a trouble-maker. The boy shifted uncomfortably and she noticed with concern that he held his right arm with his left in order to raise it from the bench. She turned her head and met a knowing look in the gentleman's eyes. The child was injured.

'I would be happy to have you sit in

on this lesson, sir. What name may I use to introduce you to the class?' she asked, meaning with even greater determination to protect the boy from Peter when the class ended. She felt sure her visitor would assist.

'Longreach,' the man said quickly. He crossed the front of the room and sat down beside Peter, who had retreated to the far corner. 'Please,' he said, and Mariah understood that tone of voice. He considered himself in charge. He was used to being in charge.

She took a levelling breath of air, such as it was in a room full of unwashed children and their filthy clothing, and began the lesson again.

* * *

Forty minutes later, the class was dismissed, and Mariah turned to look at the two men sitting in armed silence in the corner. Peter's features were set with fury. She guessed that he was feeling that his status as the presiding male was being undermined by the visitor. Mr Longreach, she was less able to understand. He smiled at her, and when Peter picked up his hateful cane he stretched an arm across it.

'I think I will be able to deal with your miscreant,' he said, and walked down the room to where the boy was the only child left. 'Tell me,' he said quietly to him, 'have you injured your arms?'

'It weren't my fault, your lordship, that it weren't. I didn't mean to charge into the gentleman,' the boy spluttered.

'Can you lift your arms?' Longreach asked.

'No, your lordship.'

'Wait outside for me, if you would. I think one of my servants may be able to help you.'

Peter was on his feet in an instant and Mariah wondered whether he would chase after the child, but he turned his ire on Mr Longreach.

'How dare you walk in here, where

you have neither interest nor occupation, and interfere with the conduct of Miss Fox's class? If I do not maintain discipline on her behalf, these louts will run wild like the pig you rescued her from last week when fortune brought you to the spot.'

'I beg your pardon, sir, it is by no means my intention to disrupt Miss Fox's class; and if you would cast your mind back a half-hour or so, you would remember that I sought her permission before observing her teaching.' Longreach moved gracefully across the floor and closed the door into the passage. 'I see much admirable work being done here, but I also see that the boy in question is seriously injured, and I think I know how it happened. He has probably suffered a dislocated shoulder and is unable to raise his hand.'

'That would certainly explain it,' Mariah said. 'He attends regularly and I do feel he is on the verge of understanding the alphabet.'

'That must be a particular delight for you, Miss Fox.'

'Yes, it is, sir, a very particular delight. When once an older boy gets to grips with the order of the letters, and if he is a good boy like this one, he will take time to help his friends or little brothers do the same.'

Her visitor smiled and she made a mental check. Aristocrats affected to be bored by everything. The boy had called him 'your lordship' in his confusion, but Mariah thought it might turn out to be true. If so, he must find her enthusiasm gauche.

'Well, well, Miss Fox. I should like to advance your ideas. May I send my mother to call on you and your papa?' he asked.

'That would be delightful. I will take great pleasure in explaining my theories to her,' she replied.

'As to that, Miss Fox, you must not expect to be able to do too much talking on first meeting my mama,' Mr Longreach said, and his smile broke into a grin that tempted Mariah to laugh. 'Sir,' he said, and executed a tight bow which Peter reluctantly matched. 'Good morning, Miss Fox.' Longreach extended a hand and shook Mariah's. 'I have enjoyed watching your skills, and I will see the boy has the best attention and a good meal or two.'

★   ★   ★

The room seemed darker and colder after Mr Longreach departed, and Mariah had to force herself into movement. The chapel's servants would clear up the beakers and sweep the crumbs, but she needed to pack her teaching materials.

'He is not honest,' Peter said. 'The boy recognised him.'

'Do you think so? I think the children will always add to supposed rank in order to earn favour, but if he is a lord, what does it matter? He may be about to offer funds to assist my classes.' She ignored Peter's knowing look and finished her tidying quickly.

She watched Peter pack the cane into his carpet-bag of books and pamphlets. He waited for her by the door, and, when she would have passed through, laid a hand on her arm.

'You have not been very much in the world, Mariah,' he said. 'I wish you to take care over your relations with this man and never to let him catch you alone.'

'Your care for me does you credit, but you must remember I have a father and an uncle. As to my supposed cloistered upbringing, I think there will be few women of Mr Longreach's class who have been into the places I have been into and seen the things I have seen.' She shrugged off his restraining hand and stepped into the street. Shivers of irritation racked her. She must make Papa understand. Peter Sharp had to be stood down as her chaperone. She could bear his presence no longer.

3

The following day, Mariah watched with surprise as Tilly backed into the big room on the ground floor. She loved this morning room because it caught the sun, and at the back, its floor-to-ceiling windows looked out over the garden and onto a small central park shared by the owners of the houses around it.

Mariah came to her feet and rescued the tray Tilly was carrying before it crashed to the ground. She put it onto a side table and wondered momentarily why the girl was bringing in their meagre supply of ratafia and Madeira. Was her papa expecting a lady visitor? She glanced affectionately at the top of his head where it was visible above *The Times*. He didn't always remember to tell her.

'Sorry, Miss Mariah,' the young

woman said. 'I'm a bit behind with things this morning as we ain't got no replacement for that last boot-boy.'

'No,' Mariah agreed. 'There's no hurry, Tilly. Papa and I can feed the fire in here when it needs coal.'

'I know, Miss, and I don't know 'ow as me and Cook would get through everything if you wasn't so easy to deal with, but I thought you'd like to see this card wot the Lady has 'ad handed in. She's waiting in 'er carriage to see if you will receive 'er.' Tilly released the embossed visiting card she had between her finger and thumb into Mariah's hand.

'Constanzia, Countess of Mellon',' Mariah read. She crossed the room and stepped into the front-window bay where she could see a large town carriage drawn up in front of the house.

'Papa,' she said, turning back, and the unaccustomed sharpness in her tone made that gentleman lower his newspaper. 'Papa, there is a carriage with a crest on the door panels drawn

44

up outside, and the Countess of Mellon has sent in her card. Did you not think to inform me we were expecting such a distinguished guest?'

The newspaper rustled as Mr Fox rose to his full height. His shoulders were stooped as a result of age and the habits of a lifetime that kept him at his desk for long hours, but he was still a tall man.

'I know no one of that name, my dear, and I have much work still to do on my pamphlet for the League of Lady Reformers. It's to be delivered within their meeting in ten days' time.' Mariah admired the rapidity of thought that had allowed him to create such an impeccable excuse from so little.

'I thought you were going to deliver the paper you wrote last year for the Association of the Wives of Manufacturers,' she said sweetly. Dearly as she loved her parent, she could see no reason she should allow him to abandon her when she was most in need of support.

'Did I?' Jerome said shiftily, and Mariah knew he was going to leave her in sole charge of this visit. 'Perhaps, but I think now that several of the ladies will be in both organisations and I do not wish to bore them. Particularly,' he added slyly, 'as they intend to donate funds to your urchins' class.'

'I found that decanter in the hall cupboard, Miss Mariah, and poured the last of the ratafia into it,' Tilly interrupted her employer, looking meaningfully at him although ostensibly speaking to Mariah.

'Undoubtedly you think it time I made a visit to my wine merchant, Tilly?' Jerome asked testily. Mariah knew he found it irksome to deal with anything not related to his educational interests and she sometimes had to visit the wine merchant herself.

'Goodness, how long has this countess been waiting, Tilly, if you've been rooting around in cupboards?' Mariah asked.

Tilly was pre-occupied with her

employer's shortfalls and took little notice. 'Cider ain't suitable for all your visitors, sir, especially when it's been drunk or stolen by the boot-boy.'

'We hardly have any visitors, Tilly,' Mariah chided gently over her shoulder as she stole another glance at the carriage. 'And you know how Mr Fox feels about the effects of strong liquors. Papa,' she said, turning back to him.

'He's escaped, Miss Mariah, escaped,' Tilly said, and Mariah felt the cool draught as the door into the back hall swung closed. 'Will you see the lady, Miss?'

★ ★ ★

Mariah was still teasing out the lace embellishment on the neck of her dress when she heard Tilly's feet patter across the tiles in the front hall. The forward door of the morning room swung open and Mariah advanced toward the exquisitely-dressed woman who came through it. She was followed by another so like her that she had to be her daughter.

'The Countess of Mellon, Miss Mariah,' Tilly said in suitably dignified tones such as Mariah had not heard her use before. 'Miss Mellon,' she added, and escaped. No doubt to regale Cook with a detailed description of these two fashionable and very, very beautiful women, Mariah thought.

Mariah dropped respectful curtsies to her visitors, and when she rose, found herself captured by the deep brown gaze of the younger woman. It was the same deep brown that had troubled her sleep through the previous night, and driven her restless from her bed to an early-morning walk around the dew-soaked gardens.

'You are his sister,' she blurted, before discretion could prevent her.

'Miss Fox,' the older woman said, ignoring her outburst. 'It is very kind of you to allow us to make this visit.' The countess was a very small person indeed and Mariah had to look down to return her gaze.

Bringing her scattered wits under control, Mariah nodded. These ladies were undoubtedly the mother and sister of the gentleman who had saved her from falling and visited her class yesterday. Her suspicions were proved right. He was an aristocrat. She shook her head and began to assemble her society manners. They were little-used or -needed, and Aunt Augusta's contributions to her upbringing had not included morning calls from anyone other than her exclusive circle of ladies associated with the blue-stocking persuasion.

It was presumably usual to invite the ladies to sit, and to offer them some of the ratafia. Mariah did ask them to sit but decided against the ratafia. There was no possibility of assessing its age, and she did not wish to be responsible for poisoning anyone.

The countess spoke again, and Mariah realised with a jolt that she had an accent. Not French, as was still common in London after the troubles in their country and the wars with Napoleon, but perhaps Spanish.

'Forgive me, Miss Fox, but I find you are very tall for a lady,' the Countess said. 'I wonder if this has attracted my son's attention to you.'

'Perhaps he thinks height adds gravitas to my presence,' she ventured.

'Gravitas?' the countess repeated in puzzled tones. 'I myself have been Countess of Mellon for thirty-two years, and I have never had any problem securing the respect and attention my position demands.'

'And Mama is not over four feet ten inches tall, Miss Fox. It's her Spanish ancestry,' the younger visitor said.

'Miss Mellon . . . '

'Actually, it's Lady Daisy, being the daughter of an earl, but as I'm certain we're going to be excellent friends, I insist you call me Daisy.' The girl rushed the words out and Mariah was not surprised when her mama intervened.

'Katerina Grizelda Anne Di Torres

are the baptismal names available to my daughter, Miss Fox, but she chooses to be known by a name that she overheard in the pantry.' The countess uttered the words in sharp staccato, and Mariah had no trouble understanding that she attracted all the respect she required be paid to her as countess.

Daisy smiled and Mariah did, too, despite the heat this argument clearly roused between her visitors. It was understandable that the older woman deplored her daughter's choice, but on the other hand, she had the demeanour and vivacity Mariah could more easily associate with *Daisy* than *Katerina Grizelda Anne Di Torres*.

'It is not obvious at our births, I believe, what the dominant traits of our personality will be,' she said diplomatically. 'Perhaps Lady Daisy feels the weight of history and expectation carried by her formal names to be too much for such delicate shoulders.'

'Daisy, please,' the younger woman said. 'But it is acknowledged by even the sour-faced tabbies at Almack's that I have very delicate shoulders.'

'Daisy, I feel we have allowed your exuberance enough freedom,' the countess said, and Mariah watched with fascination as the younger girl slid back into the cushions behind her. Clearly, when her mama adopted a certain tone, she knew she had overstepped her licence to behave in the flighty manner she believed attractive. Mariah thought she detected a little disappointment in the girl's expression, and another thought stole through her brain: Perhaps Lady Daisy Mellon is not as feather-brained as she might be judged on her performance. Perhaps she simply hid a natural intelligence? She would not be unusual among her class in doing so, since they believed intelligence in a woman to be a disadvantage in attracting a husband.

'I can see what has attracted my son to you, Miss Fox. You will deal well with those obnoxious people one meets in the country,' the countess said, and

Mariah sat up straighter. What an odd remark for the woman to make. Was the family looking to appoint a teacher rather than simply invest in the classes she was already running?

'May I ask, ma'am, if we are indeed talking about the gentleman who rescued me from the certain prospect of a head injury?' Mariah asked.

'Tobias said nothing about head injuries, Miss Fox. He said you were a teacher, and as my need is very great and my circumstances becoming most pressing, I did not inquire,' Lady Mellon said. 'Have you suffered a head injury?'

'No, ma'am, your son stepped forward very quickly, and, er . . . and lifted me out of danger.' Mariah stifled her embarrassment.

'Tobias is the Earl of Mellon, Miss Fox,' Daisy said, unable to maintain her silence any longer. 'He did not introduce himself? I see he did not. He can be very remiss.'

'No,' Mariah said quietly, 'he did

introduce himself to my companion and me, but as Mr Longreach.' She was unsure why she had mentioned Peter's existence, but thought perhaps it was important that the countess did not believe she wandered about in dubious areas unaccompanied.

'We are here now,' Lady Mellon said, 'and I find that, although I am surprised to have you thrust into my life, I can see why Tobias does so. It will relieve my mind greatly, Miss Fox, if you take on the position.'

'There is a position?' Mariah asked. Did she want to take on any more teaching? Would it involve leaving Papa and moving to the country? She was unsure if she could do that.

'Certainly, it is a position,' Lady Mellon said, and Mariah heard the strain that imbued the words. How could a lady of such standing be so in need of a humble teacher? 'It is a position and you will need to understand fully what will be required of you. There can be no backing out once you have agreed to take it on.'

'Mama,' Daisy began but was interrupted by the doorbell clanging loudly in the hall. 'Why,' she said startled, 'it does not ring in the servants' hall.'

'It does,' Mariah said without mentioning that they had only the kitchen downstairs, 'but because we have so few staff and they are not always here overnight, I had another bell installed in the upstairs hall.'

Daisy regarded her speculatively and Mariah felt sure there was more than a little mischief sparking from the girl's eyes. She watched with a dread fascination as the visitor turned to face the door in frank anticipation of who might come through it. We are freaks, Mariah thought despairingly. Even this lively and friendly girl cannot truly understand what it would be like to lift the latch on one's own front door.

Matters were bad enough, but the new arrival was set to make them much worse. Tilly's voice could be heard in the hall, valiantly trying to send Peter

Sharp upstairs to Papa's bolt-hole. She did not win.

'Mr Sharp, Miss Mariah,' the girl said, and raised her eyebrows meaningfully. Clearly she realises how this is going to deteriorate, Mariah thought. She stood up and advanced on Peter before he was fully into the room.

'Peter,' she said, as calmly as she could, although her stomach churned with nervous agitation. 'Papa is upstairs working on his paper for the League of Lady Reformers. I am sure he would appreciate any pointers you might make on it.'

Peter sketched a tiny bow and Mariah knew he was still smarting from his dismissal the previous afternoon. He straightened and looked past her to study the two ladies making such elegant splashes of colour in the home where visitors usually wore undyed woollen garments of no colour and no particular cut. Mariah saw a combative light flash into his pale eyes. No doubt he recognised the resemblance between the women, and the family likeness to Mr Longreach.

'I think not, Mariah.' Peter adopted his most officious tone. 'Your papa finished that paper three days ago. Is it not the case that he has removed himself from the present company lest he suffer boredom?'

Mariah bridled. How dare he insult her guests without any knowledge of them, or familiarity with their conversation?

'I am sure Papa had no such thought in mind. He is not, as you know well, the most sociable of creatures.' It was impossible to attempt any introduction to the countess following his rudeness, and she did not do so. The best she could hope to achieve would be to see the ladies out before he further damned them all in their eyes.

'My lady, it has been a great pleasure to entertain you this morning,' she said, and turned from the countess. 'And also you, Lady Daisy.'

The countess rose to her full stature

and smoothed the folds of her pale-lilac walking gown. She glanced at her daughter, who rose too, and moved across the room to stand beside Mariah. Mariah felt a surge of warmth, as though the girl's closeness brought with it support and reassurance.

Lady Mellon inclined her head to Mariah and walked from the room. Daisy hung back a little and fixed her piercing brown gaze on Peter's smug countenance. They all waited, and in seconds, uncertain colour flushed across his cheeks.

'I think this must be the man who was supposed to be escorting you yesterday, Miss Fox,' Lady Daisy said. 'I recognise him from the earl's description: too old, too fat, and too stupid.'

Mariah breathed deeply lest she faint. Social niceties could be readily abandoned by anyone, it seemed. She heard Tilly's hasty cough in the hall and knew it was covering a snort of laughter, such as she made when the baker's boy stopped by in the kitchen.

'Mama is well pleased with you, I can tell. You may call at the house tomorrow morning at noon, if that is suitable for your arrangements,' Lady Daisy said, and the words drew Mariah's startled gaze to her. 'Our town address is on the back of Mama's card.'

'Noon? Yes, I think noon is suitable,' Mariah replied. 'However, I may not be able to take up any position that involves leaving Papa.'

'All the Mellon properties are big enough to accommodate your papa, Miss Fox.' Daisy swept from the room.

'Well, Mariah, it seems my fears were more than justified,' Peter said, grinding the words in irritation.

'Fears? Perhaps 'hopes' better fits the circumstances. The campaign is always in need of funds, and Mr Longreach . . . '

'The Earl of Mellon! I warned you he was not honest. The aristocracy think only of themselves and their parasitical families. They are not fit associates for a woman like you. I must speak to Jerome

59

about this,' he finished, and strode from the room.

Mariah stared at the empty air where Peter had been. He had not been so animated in her presence ever before. Apparently, Papa had correctly read signs she had not recognised. Mariah knew it was time to avoid being alone with Peter Sharp. She hoped to marry one day, and when she did, it would be for the love of another human being, not because she had sleepwalked into familiarity.

4

The following morning, Tobias waited just along the mews, where he had a good view into Grosvenor Square and back to the way he thought Mariah Fox would walk from her home in Redde Place. He was sure she would walk and he was sure she would come. If challenged, he would not be able to give any explanation of this conviction, but conviction it was.

At three minutes to noon he saw her and drew himself up to his full height. His papa had been a tall man, and despite his mama's tiny frame, Tobias topped six feet by two or more inches. It was a disadvantage to be quite so tall when seeking dancing partners. Mariah Fox was a tall girl who would not be swamped by his height should he take her onto the dance floor.

'Good morning, Miss Fox,' he said

when they arrived at Mellon House's entrance stairs at the same moment. 'This is a most pleasant surprise.'

'Is it?' she replied, unsmiling, and Tobias began to think he may have made one or two misjudgements in his plan to captivate Miss Fox. 'Is it not your hand behind the changes taking place in my life?'

'I did ask my mama to make a morning call, as I said I would. I would not have your family think I intend anything underhand towards you, Miss Fox,' he said and watched, intrigued, as a flash of temperament sparkled in the blue of her eyes.

'Your mama made herself very clear. I was the answer to her problem in filling a difficult position that involved being diplomatic to obnoxious persons in the country. However, I am very much afraid that Lady Daisy insulted Mr Sharp, the gentleman who was my escort when you attended my class, and my papa is not . . . ' She straggled to a stop, and her blue eyes studied him intently. 'I will descend the basement stairs and ring the servants' bell, Lord Mellon. Forgive me for taking up your valuable time.'

Tobias stepped to the side as Mariah made to cross the pavement and go down into the basement area. For what position had his mama said she was going to be considered? He did not think it would be appropriate for the future countess — which was the position he had made it clear to his mama *he* was considering in relation to Miss Fox — to make her first arrival in the house through the servants' corridors. But if Daisy had implied that the position was that of teacher in the estate school, then he could see why she was so intent on keeping to her place. A lady in that position in life would not wish to seem encroaching.

'I fear there has been a little mischief-making going on. Where my sister is involved, that is only to be expected, Miss Fox. I hope Mr Sharp will recover from any affront in time,' he said. He extended an arm to prevent her setting foot on the basement stairs, aware she would not refuse an earl on his doorstep.

She laid her fingers delicately, almost diffidently, on his arm. He turned her toward the front entrance and, when she would have resisted, urged her forward.

'The main door, my lord? I am sure this cannot be what your mama had in mind when she asked me to call for an interview,' she said, and Tobias was further captivated by the mellifluous tones. How could any urchin be indifferent to the alphabet when it was enunciated so eloquently? She offered no simpering uncertainties but a clear statement of her feelings.

'And Mr Sharp is unlikely to recover from the *affront*, as you term it,' she added.

'Then I must conclude Daisy repeated my description of Mr Sharp in full,' he said regretfully.

'Too old, too fat, and too stupid'

were the words, my lord. They are unkind and also untrue,' she said.

Tobias weighed up the matter and decided honesty was best with this young lady. 'You cannot be more than twenty-one, Miss Fox, and I think Mr Sharp is perhaps in his middle forties. In exceptional cases — my parents, for example — this may work to the advantage of both parties; but in the ordinary case . . . ' He shrugged. 'In the ordinary case, it is not wise to have such a wide age gap. 'Too fat'? How can you argue, ma'am? 'Too stupid'? I think you will trot out a list of his accomplishments, but they will all be nullified by his threat to take a cane to a child already suffering pain.'

'How is the boy?'

'His shoulder had been dislocated and my groom has put it back. With a sling protecting it and several bowls of Cook's broth inside him, he is perking up,' Tobias said, watching the conflicting emotions roused by this tale cross Miss Fox's face. 'His name is Josh.'

'Thank you, my lord.' A fleeting smile warmed her features, but was soon replaced as she returned to the subject of the miserable Peter Sharp. 'An argument ensued after the ladies' visit, which has caused a breach with my papa. I should perhaps mention that Papa regarded Mr Sharp as my intended,' Mariah said calmly.

'Your intended, Miss Fox? I had thought that matters did not stand in such condition between you and Mr Sharp. I apologise without reserve if I have caused you any distress.' He stood very still, waiting for her reply. He realised it would be the most important speech of his life to date.

Mariah drew a shallow breath and kept her eyes lowered. The brim of the new chip-straw bonnet she and Tilly had purchased yesterday afternoon made it easy to avoid looking straight at his lordship should she not wish to do so. She did not wish to do so, of course, because she was here to discuss a position with his mama, the countess, and it would not serve to be always looking at him.

She pulled a mental brake on her thoughts. They were galloping ahead and very likely to get out of control. In truth, there was every prospect she would never see his lordship again, even if she agreed to take on the position. His interest was undoubtedly in helping his mama to secure the best person for a troublesome vacancy.

'I do not wish to discuss my affairs, sir, beyond what your mama needs to know in order to select the best person for her teaching position,' she said with a touch of asperity. Why should it hurt so much that Lord Mellon was being solicitous only in his anxiety not to spoil his mama's chances of securing her services?

'My mama has no interest at all in selecting persons for teaching positions, Miss Fox,' the earl said. 'Whatever her eccentricities, she has always left the employment of staff to those better-suited and better-qualified to do so.'

'Then why have I been invited here?' Mariah asked. A horrible thought crossed her mind. 'I would not consider working as a paid companion,' she blurted out. 'My papa is able to support me.' She cast a startled glance at the earl, whose burst of laughter shook the ribbons on her new bonnet.

'Companion? No. My mama is the most demanding of ladies, but she and her companion have rubbed along now for thirty years, and are likely to do so until one of them dies. Besides, you may not speak Spanish, which Mama insists on in her leisure hours,' the earl said, and urged her onto the steps of the house.

'Then why am I here, Lord Mellon?' Mariah demanded, but then the butler opened the door and bowed his master over the threshold, preventing any reply. As she looked from the butler to the surrounding area, her eyes widened in shock. She had never been within a building of such elegance and refinement.

The hall was painted in pale blue with an ornate cornice picked out in darker blue and ivory. There were a few upright chairs with the family crest carved into their backs, and one long mahogany table set back against the facing wall. The central part rose through four stories to a glass copula in the roof. In front of them, a staircase enticed the gaze up to a wide carpeted landing from which several doors no doubt led into the house's public rooms.

Mariah gathered her scattered wits. Any family that could keep this building as its London home would indeed be able to accommodate her papa as well as herself. How naive she must seem to Lord Mellon with her insistent questions about positions. She must calm herself and go to his mama with an open mind. This family would have many interests and might be looking for a way to spend their money on furthering philanthropic causes. She must do nothing to deflect any such interest. Funds and access to suitable premises were of paramount importance in furthering the cause of universal education. The Mellon family clearly had both.

'We will go up to Mama, Stephens,' the earl said.

At her side, the butler bowed and Mariah offered a small smile, which he ignored. A maid appeared from behind him and dropped a curtsy.

'May I help you with your spencer, miss?' she asked, and Mariah undid the buttons to slide the garment off her arms. She watched the girl carry away her new bonnet and sighed. It had been a major purchase but, as she looked around, she could not regret spending her entire month's pin money on it. She wished her pale green morning gown were of silk and not serviceable cotton, but there was nothing she could do to alter that. Besides, it was her most attractive gown, and pale green suited her fair skin.

She lifted her head and turned from

the maid to find Lord Mellon's gaze fixed on her with an intensity that would have made her blush, had she forgotten the difference in their social stations. She would not forget. No matter that Lady Mellon had condescended to come to Redde Place and sit in their morning room. She would not forget.

Lord Mellon gestured to the elegant staircase and they went up to the first floor, following the butler. Stephens led them into a drawing room and announced them both.

'Such formality,' Mariah said involuntarily, and heard her companion suppress a chuckle.

'It's as nothing compared with the state my grandmother insisted on,' he whispered. 'My elder brother and I were forever wiping our faces and hands until they were deemed clean enough.' The shared joke drew her to him in her nervousness, and she sent him a grateful smile.

'Good morning, Miss Fox,' the

countess said as she stood to receive her visitors. 'Tobias, what brings you abroad at such an early hour?'

'This criticism is unfair, Mama,' the earl said, and he advanced to kiss his parent. 'I am frequently abroad a deal earlier.'

'But you do not choose to visit your mother,' the countess continued. 'No matter. You are here now and we may hope to enjoy your company. Miss Fox, please sit here.'

Mariah moved across the room, conscious of all eyes following her progress. She had noticed an older woman sitting to one side and supposed she would be the countess's companion. Lady Daisy sat moodily on a window seat, and a young man of some bulk and a florid complexion, who had been sitting with her, rose as the countess did. He now left Daisy and crossed towards the group gathering around the fireplace.

There was already a footman, who seemed to be waiting to offer cold drinks, in the room, and the butler stationed himself beside him.

Lord Mellon allowed his mama to resume her seat and then turned to Lady Daisy's companion, whose heavy breathing filled the otherwise silent room with noise.

'John, I see you have made an early visit as well,' the earl said, and Mariah picked up a tone of mild censure. She wondered if this interplay between the men had anything to do with Lady Daisy, but resisted the urge to turn to that young person and meet eyes that would no doubt be full of expression. Lord Mellon was making an introduction, and she smiled before dropping a curtsy to his friend, Mr John Brent.

'Mr Brent was just taking his leave,' Daisy said, and moved into the circle. 'He finds his tailor requires his presence urgently.'

'On the contrary, Lady Daisy,' Brent said with a slight flush that faded quickly, 'I would trespass on Lady

Mellon's hospitality a few more minutes.' He acknowledged that lady's nod and waited for Daisy to take a seat before positioning himself to one side of Mariah's chair. 'I have been keenly interested to make your acquaintance, Miss Fox, since I missed doing so by a whisker last Tuesday morning. Have you long had an interest in teaching children?'

'Yes, Mr Brent. I have been involved with educational pursuits since I was fifteen years old and first tried my hand at my own former school. I find I have a small talent that encourages children to pay attention,' she said.

Inwardly, she wondered if Mr Brent had been invited to conduct her interview, and was careful how she replied to his questions. She had some experience of appearing before panels of ladies who might donate money towards finding premises and materials for her urchin schools in the industrial areas. Those occasions were often conducted in church halls or similar, and she felt a tiny smile touch her mouth when she thought of the difference in surroundings.

'And would you wish to continue your work with these children, Miss Fox, after your marriage?' the countess interrupted. 'The duties of any married woman are great, it need not be said, but the duties of a woman in the position you would find yourself are all-encompassing.'

'I beg your pardon, my lady, I had not thought of marrying in the near future. I know it must seem a little strange that Mr Sharp acts as my escort, but he is like an uncle in our household,' Mariah said, crossing her fingers below the reticule on her lap.

'An uncle, hmm?' the earl murmured, and Mariah was unable to meet his eyes. 'I am relieved to hear that.'

'Mr Sharp? Tobias, you did not think to mention that the young woman's affections might be engaged elsewhere?' the countess enquired, her voice rising in a panic and becoming more accented. 'I have been waiting for eight or more years to wish you happy. Am I to be frustrated by some Mr Sharp?'

Mariah rose from her chair as astonishment over the countess's words ripped through her brain. She sank into it again lest she spill the glass of sweet wine being offered to her by the butler. Automatically, she took the slender stem in her gloved hand. It shook.

'Mama, you are causing a great deal of distress to our visitor,' Lord Mellon said, and Mariah felt a strong hand extricate the glass from her fingers and set it onto a side table.

'Distress! There are few mothers in this land who have experienced as much distress as I,' the countess exclaimed, and Mariah heard Daisy's quick sigh.

'Calmly, Mama, please try to stay calm,' Lord Mellon said.

'Tobias, I visited this young lady yesterday at your behest,' the countess said.

Mariah heard John Brent's interested murmur of 'Really!' at her side.

'I was subjected to the insolence of a visiting male who implied that your sister and I had less than a brain between us. You are now telling me to be calm,' the countess added with indignation, as colour suffused her olive complexion. Then she lifted a book from her side table and threw it with remarkably fine aim at her son.

'Oh, I say, ma'am. I always wondered how Toby came to be such a fine bowler. He clearly inherits his eye from you,' John Brent said, and must instantly have regretted his interference because Lady Mellon lifted another volume and threw it, too, catching him on the shoulder.

Mariah heard a rustle of skirts behind her, and the lady she had earlier identified as the countess's companion came forward, speaking soothingly in Spanish. Within a few moments, she and Stephens had led the countess from the room and the young people remained alone.

'Do sit down, Mr Brent. You are looming,' Daisy snapped.

'Indeed, Lady Daisy, I would not wish to loom over you, and will take my leave. As you said earlier, a pressing engagement with my tailor calls to me. Toby, forgive me, but I will hope to catch up with you at White's. Miss Fox.' John Brent turned to her and made a neat bow before saying, 'It has been an enormous pleasure to make your acquaintance.'

★   ★   ★

Tobias waited until the door closed behind his friend and the footman before he came back to sit down with Daisy and Mariah. He found it impossible to tell whether Mariah was shocked most by his mama's behaviour or by that lady's revelation — that she expected them to become betrothed.

'Miss Fox,' he began, but when the girl raised her head the condemnation in her blue eyes killed the words of reassurance in his throat. He would have to work very hard if he wanted to recover his standing with her.

'Lord Mellon,' Mariah said, and stood up. Tobias watched her straighten the drape of her morning gown and thought the colour was an excellent choice for a lady with such fair skin. 'I am astonished by all that has passed here this morning. I believed I was summoned to be interviewed for a post as a teacher among country persons your mama described as obnoxious. I now see she was talking, not about children, but about her neighbours.'

'Miss Fox . . . ' Tobias began again, but discovered that not every young lady in the land was impressed into silence by his title, his situation as a bachelor, and his access to immense wealth, because Miss Fox cast him a glance so full of loathing he felt its heat sear through to his brain.

'I am full of contrition, Miss Fox, and beg your pardon for exposing you to so much unexpected behaviour,' he said at last. The expression of anger in those wonderful eyes did not lessen by any measurable quantity. 'You must wonder at Lady Mellon's distress, but it is brought about by too strict an adherence to her beliefs in the attentions needed by an adult son. She wishes to go to Spain and live for a while with her relatives . . . '

'And to speak Spanish all the time,' Daisy added from her chair.

'To this end, she sees it as necessary that I should be married before she departs on her odyssey,' Tobias concluded, and watched Mariah Fox carefully to assess whether she would grasp his problem and understand why he had moved with such indecent haste.

'I have never been subjected to such an insult, sir. We met last week for fewer than ten minutes, and two days ago for an hour. How dare you make sport of me in this manner?' Mariah asked, and despite the strength of his purpose, he felt his heart constrict. He had acted like a soldier, seizing the chance that fate threw to him without any regard to the feelings of those involved.

'I do not make sport, Miss Fox. I wish to be married in order to release my mama from her obligations, and I consider being married to you as an excellent solution for us all,' he said. 'I realise, albeit a little late in the proceedings, that I have moved too quickly for everyone concerned. My mama was not supposed to reveal any of this, but to act with all courtesy and attention to you. It was never my intention to have any of this blurted out, particularly in front of John Brent.'

'Is Mr Brent a noted gossip?' Mariah asked. 'Does he entertain himself by sending snippets of information about his friends to the newspapers?'

'I hope I choose my friends with greater care,' Tobias snapped. Too late, he remembered Miss Fox had every reason to believe she was the injured party. How could she know he was simply embarrassed to be proving

John's assumption of his interest in her? 'I do beg your pardon, Miss Fox,' he said contritely.

'Toby believed Mama would be able to keep the intention behind her visit to you a secret and await developments,' Daisy said. 'I think that only a man could have believed such piffle.' She snorted with hysterical laughter.

'That noise would not have been out of place among the stable lads,' Tobias said coldly. He cursed the needs of propriety that would not allow him to eject his sister. He had enough ground to recover where Miss Fox was concerned without compromising her by shutting them in the drawing room alone.

Mariah turned toward Daisy, but the glacier blue of her eyes did not alter by much. 'You seemed to be fully conversant with the 'piffle', however, Lady Daisy,' she said. 'I commend you on your powers of dissimulation. No doubt they were reinforced by the desire to observe how we went on in our house with its bell in the hall.'

Tobias found this remark quite mystifying, but he noticed with satisfaction that it had hit home where his sister was concerned. She rose instantly and made a curtsy to Mariah.

'Miss Fox, I am mortified that you should believe I would want to make fun of your circumstances. I do beg your understanding. Toby and Mama are formidable personalities when one is a daughter entirely dependent on their goodwill,' she said, and while she allowed a slight tremble to be heard in her voice, she did not make the mistake of noisy tears. Tobias was sure Miss Fox would see through that in an instant.

'I understand the nature of dependency only too well, Lady Daisy,' Mariah said. 'I am also terrifyingly well-educated, and sadly able to recognise the mendacious nature of your remarks,' she added without heat, before turning and walking away from them.

***

Mariah gripped her reticule so tightly flashes of pain stung her hands but she welcomed the distraction they made because they prevented her bursting into shameful tears. All she wished for was to make her way down to the front hall and leave. She would not wait for her spencer or her new bonnet. She would leave.

Lord Mellon crossed the vast carpeted space in an instant and reached the double doors of the drawing room before she set foot on the wooden surround. She breathed in, and his smell filled her being with scents of sandalwood and horse. Perhaps he had visited his stables before arranging to loiter in the street as she arrived. No doubt he had worked out that she would have to come alone, as her papa would not be persuaded to accompany her the short distance which divided their vastly separate worlds, if it took him away from his books and preparations.

They descended the staircase in militant silence and Mariah saw the maid who had attended her on arrival, waiting at its foot with her spencer and bonnet. For a moment she wondered if the poor child had spent the last half-hour standing there, but soon saw she was out of breath and had probably been summoned by a listening footman. The thought provided yet further mortification. Did all the staff know she had been placed in the position she found herself?

'Letty will help you with your things,' Lord Mellon said, and Mariah allowed herself to be dressed for her departure. What had persuaded her to come to this place where her cotton gown made her as conspicuous as a flowering weed in an herbaceous border? Pride, she decided, and arrogance; for she was not one to excuse her own follies.

She had not paid sufficient attention to Peter Sharp's warnings about the nature of the aristocracy. She had persuaded herself that these aristocrats had philanthropic aims in their dealings with her.

'I will accompany you back to Redde Place,' Lord Mellon said, and Mariah stepped back.

'That will not be necessary, Lord Mellon. It is less than ten minutes' walk and my appearance is not such as will attract footpads or young bucks,' she said tartly, refusing to acknowledge her appearance had attracted Lord Mellon himself a week ago.

'That's as may be, Miss Fox, but I insist,' he replied. 'Letty, you will attend Miss Fox.'

The girl blushed with pleasure to be directly addressed by her master. It made Mariah angrier than she had been. The girl's position was so servile an order delivered without a smile or a 'please' should make her so pleased. She opened her mouth to make an acerbic comment but was silenced by the fierceness of Lord Mellon's glare.

'Good,' he said as he strode toward

the open front door. 'I see you have reflected on your reputation, which would not be enhanced by being seen alone with me.'

'You are ordering this child around for my benefit?' she asked. 'How dare you?'

'I believe I employ Letty and her time is mine to dispose as I see fit,' he said, and for the first time she heard irritation creep into his tone. Good; she was making an impression that she could be proud of. She was making him think about the inequalities of life.

'And no doubt the housekeeper will have her kept from her dinner until she completes whatever task she had set Letty before you hauled her away from it,' Mariah challenged.

'You cannot be aware of how a great house operates, Miss Fox,' he said, but did not stop to allow her the chance to intervene. 'My housekeeper assigned Letty to your needs. She will not be ground into exhaustion filling coal scuttles on her return. I would not presume to interfere with the running of Mrs. Burtles's empire.'

'Nor I with Cook's,' she said involuntarily, and turned startled eyes to his. The fierceness had mellowed into something like understanding and she quickened her pace.

'So, Miss Fox, you are able to find similarities in our positions?' he asked, and his voice was not without kindness, but she knew he was feeling a little triumphant to have caught her out.

'I do not believe that my papa's cook and the housekeeper of your residence have a great deal in common,' she said.

'Miss Fox, had I not caused you so much discomfiture this morning already, it would be my duty to call you to task for uttering such a monstrous falsehood,' he replied, and now he was laughing at her.

The realisation inflamed her raw nerves and she stopped in the middle of the concourse, to the consternation of an elderly gentleman and his wife who could not manoeuvre quickly enough and crashed into Letty. Lord Mellon was obliged to pick her up as he had lifted Mariah, and the girl froze in his arms.

'Are you unharmed, Letty?' he asked. He set the girl on her feet and watched as she tidied the shawl loosened by her fall.

'Yes, m'lord,' Letty mumbled and straightened up. 'I be fine, sir.'

'I am very sorry, Letty,' Mariah said. 'I was not careful enough.'

'I be fine, miss. I be fine to go on with you and the master.' Mariah realised she was worried in case either of her superiors thought this would be a good moment to send her back to the house. She also knew Letty's position in the servants' hall would be much more comfortable for a few days while the others wrested from her the details of her walk with the master and his young lady friend. Mariah closed her eyes in momentary confusion. When had anyone ever regarded her as an object of fashionable interest?

'If you are ready, Miss Fox, we might go on,' Lord Mellon said, and Mariah fell into step at his side once more. She had ignored his arm when he proffered it on departing the mansion house, but now she laid her fingers on it. There was strength and warmth there, and if they were attracting attention from others out strolling before the luncheon hour, it was good to know they saw her in company together with the earl and not at odds with him.

5

Tobias felt the light press of Mariah Fox's fingers on his arm as they completed the walk to Redde Place. He was going over in his mind the details of his mama's lamentable loss of control. He had stressed to her that Mariah was to be visited, and invited to return the visit, without any hint being made of his intentions or the change in her circumstances he might in time bring about. He was now aware that he had not devoted enough attention to his mama's need to return to Spain. She was even closer to a collapse than he had known when he spoke with John on Tuesday.

Tobias stopped when Miss Fox did and cast a glance over the three-storey house before them. It was neat enough, and he interpreted this as a sign that Miss Fox attended to her surroundings.

He had heard of her father, and knew the gentleman was immersed in his educational plans and his own rigorous study. It was unlikely that he took any interest in his domestic arrangements.

'It is a most charming house, Miss Fox,' he said. 'I think you have chosen the plants for your window boxes very well. The colours are complimentary to the blond stone of the walls.'

'Thank you, Lord Mellon. And thank you for your escort. I am indebted,' she said, and it annoyed him unreasonably to hear her so meek and conventional. Was it returning to her father's house that had this effect?

'I liked it better when you were telling me what a villain I am,' he said.

She looked up at him then. The surprise in her eyes was obvious. 'Why should that be, sir?'

'It is more honest and more of your character.'

'To forget my manners and berate you?' she asked, but tempered the question with a smile that touched the corners of her eyes. He seized the advantage, and while she was unguarded, pressed her towards the low steps at the front of the house.

'You did not forget your manners. You were mightily provoked. I wish to explain my mama's desire to return to Spain and how I feel you could assist in achieving it. If you think your papa is in the house, may I request your permission to come in?'

'Papa will be at home,' she said, and he caught the hesitation in acceding to his request. 'I think he may have Mr Sharp with him.'

'Indeed? I understood you to say earlier that a breach in relations had occurred because of my intrusion in your lives.'

'I did say so, but it is the case that Mr Sharp does not absent himself for long over any breach,' she replied, and he understood. Whatever Miss Fox thought of Mr Sharp, he thought of her and her papa as his to command.

'The days of one gentleman calling

another out over insults are almost at an end, Miss Fox. I have no doubt hotheads will continue for several years, but I am not one of those, and from my observation of the erudite Mr Sharp, I think he is not either,' he said.

'I have no fear on that score, Lord Mellon, but Mr Sharp's displeasure can taint any atmosphere for days,' she said, and Tobias had to prevent his heart softening. This girl was made for greater things than pacifying the temper of two selfish men who believed their intellects set them apart. Someone needed to make her understand as much.

'Do you spend a great deal of your time arranging your papa's life to prevent Mr Sharp irritating him? Or indeed to prevent Mr Sharp being irritated?' he asked, and saw the flash of temper light her eyes. Good, he thought. 'If, as you have led me to believe, your aim in life is to secure education for as many as possible, then you would do better to escape from such domestic disharmony.'

'Lord Mellon,' she said quietly, 'you know nothing about the life I live unless you have been investigating me in order to make me vulnerable to your ploys.'

'I do not know as much about your life as I would wish,' he said calmly, 'and that is a state of affairs I seek to remedy. Shall we go in?'

* * *

Mariah reluctantly led the way into the house, and was not surprised to find Tilly opening the inner door as she entered the tiled vestibule. The girl had been spying through the side-light.

'Tilly, is Papa in the downstairs study?' she asked the maid, who was agog at the appearance of her escort. Mariah had forgotten how circumscribed their lives were. Of course Tilly would be interested in the earl's tailored wool coat with his spotless waistcoat and carefully-tied neck-cloth. The men who normally visited here wore ill-fitting garments which were often stained with food. Not only that, but the earl had a clean-shaven face, and the hair of his head was trimmed into a neat style that allowed his strong bones to be easily seen. Seen and admired, she thought.

'Tilly,' Mariah said, with a touch of sharpness she did not usually display.

'Yes, miss,' Tilly asked breathlessly. The girl bobbed a curtsy and then several others as she took Mariah's bonnet and the earl's walking cane and tall hat. She was about to curtsy to Letty but realised, as her feet tangled in her haste, that the girl was a servant and would mock her mistake. She sat down in a heap.

'It seems that my very presence is dangerous to any female acquainted with you, Miss Fox,' the earl said. He moved behind Tilly and in one smooth action lifted the girl onto her feet. 'Letty, we depart in twenty minutes. Miss Fox, lead on.'

Mariah's sensibilities jangled. She felt

he had mustered them like a troop of regimentals, but short of creating a pointless scene, she could only do as he asked. She opened the door of the big downstairs room and felt her spirits dampen as Peter's voice, with its intolerable tone of faint criticism, reached them. She drooped. Lord Mellon was close behind her, perhaps too close for the observance of propriety, and she felt the heat of his breath against her ear as he leaned forward to whisper into it.

'Courage, Miss Fox. You have a reserve battalion at your disposal today.'

Mariah's short laugh alerted the two men already in the room and they stood up. Peter's face flushed into dark carmine when he recognised who Mariah's escort was. Her papa cast a glance of enquiry from the elegant gentleman to his daughter.

'Lord Mellon, may I present my father, Jerome Fox,' Mariah said with as much calm as she could call to her aid. The two men exchanged polite bows.

She turned to Peter and sent him a welcoming smile, but it had no effect on his now disdainful expression. 'And his colleague, Mr Peter Sharp.' Peter and the earl exchanged bows of brittle politeness.

Mariah crossed the room and sat down on a little sofa that had been her mama's. Her papa indicated a chair to the earl, who sat down also, and waited for the others to be seated before he addressed Jerome.

'Forgive this intrusion in your morning's work, Mr Fox. I begged leave of your daughter to make an unannounced visit and she was kind enough to accommodate my wishes.'

'Really, Mariah,' Peter said, 'you must be aware how busy your papa is this week, with so much to accomplish before he is drawn into the round of lectures that raise funds to keep your classes going.' He delivered this homily as if they had been alone. Mariah checked the urge to apologise, which was second nature where her papa's work was concerned, and directed a questioning glance at Peter.

'Are you suggesting, Peter, that I am unmindful of Papa's workload?' she asked. 'Or even that I have set out to sabotage it?'

'Of course I do not suggest you meant to sabotage it. Only that the female is unable to fully enter into the results of her thoughtless and self-centred actions,' Peter said.

He wants the earl to believe I answer, not to Papa, but to him, Mariah thought.

'I am unable to agree with your assertion, Mr Sharp,' the earl said easily. 'I find that a propensity to forget actions have consequences is shared by the male and the female in equal measure. In fact, I am here this morning to explain to Miss Fox a matter concerning the consequences of my failure to address fully the probable result of one of my actions.'

'As to that, my lord, Mariah has her papa and me to act on her behalf. We need not detain her from her pre-luncheon titivations any further,' Peter said.

Mariah remained sitting with the utmost difficulty. She was a person totally opposed to the use of violence — even the accepted chastisement of children in class was abhorrent to her, and its abolition was one of her most dearly-held objectives — but nothing would have given her more satisfaction at that moment than to bring her hand across Peter's self-satisfied smirk.

'Peter, I think you forget how Mariah has been educated,' Jerome said.

'No, sir, I do not believe I do. Mariah's brain has been trained to read and figure, and her fingers to write, but I regret that the female cannot be taught logic and reasoning. It must be clear that this man, with his title and wealth, has turned her head from its true path . . . '

'I think, Peter. I speak. I am not deaf; nor, as you seem intent on implying, am I essentially feeble-minded,' Mariah said. No longer able to remain seated, she was on her feet and trembling with a cold rage that made her words flow in well-chosen phrases. 'Papa, you have welcomed Peter here as your guest, but I must tell you that if you continue to do so, I will seek a residential position in a ladies' seminary.'

'I think not, my dear,' Jerome said in some shock. 'It was difficult enough when I was a younger man, but I would find it impossible to go on without your assistance, particularly since . . . ' He drew himself to a stop, as if he had been about to say something he should not have.

Mariah frowned, but her papa continued to speak, and the moment to ask what he meant passed.

'But never mind about my ramblings.' He stood up, the better to face the younger men who had risen when Mariah did. 'Peter, I am sorry you have allowed your antipathy for Lord Mellon to overpower your sense. It would perhaps be better for all concerned if you took your leave at this time.'

'You aren't considering this matter fully, Jerome,' Peter said. Mariah realised he was not yet grasping how deeply he had offended father and daughter. 'I know you have striven to treat Mariah as you would have treated the son you were deprived of, but there is a moment when a person must accept that women are not the same as men, and this is particularly so when it comes to the assessment of character.'

'I fear you are right in this one respect, Mr Sharp. It is some time since my daughter made me aware you were not a benign influence in her teaching, and I was loath to believe matters were as serious as she indicated. I have not been a reliable judge of character.' Jerome turned to Mariah, and she was shocked by the sorrow etched in his face.

'Mariah, please ring for Tilly and ask her to show Mr Sharp out,' he said, turning to stride across to the big windows overlooking the gardens. His narrow back was rigid.

Peter took a step toward Jerome, but the earl shook his head. 'I recommend you to leave now, Mr Sharp,' he said quietly.

Mariah hoped the bell had rung in the kitchen: the mechanism didn't always work. But they soon heard Tilly's footsteps, and she gave her Jerome's instructions. She resumed her seat on the sofa and did not look at Peter Sharp again as he left the room. They heard the street door close and Tilly's footsteps patter back to the kitchen stairs.

Jerome stayed by the windows for a moment or two after, and then came slowly across the room to take his seat again. He had aged in the last hour, and Mariah felt guilty. He had quarrelled with his most faithful young protégé and it was all her fault.

'I must beg your forgiveness, Mariah. I had not thought to find Peter Sharp so devious a personality. All the while he has professed to share

103

my view that in time education must be universal, he has harboured a separate and backward-looking belief in the inferiority of the female intellect. I am devastated.'

'I am so sorry, Papa. I should not have voiced such a self-regarding threat to your happiness. I cannot think what made me do it,' Mariah said as she inwardly absorbed how devastated her father appeared.

'Come, come, my dear. What else could you have said? The man is stupid beyond what can be borne; and I was stupid, too, not to understand the baseness of his nature and the flimsy quality of his support.' Jerome plucked at the sleeve of his jacket in a manner he had used when Aunt Augusta lived with them for a time while Mr Wilson was abroad.

The earl was still on his feet and he coughed a little. Mariah started and looked to him.

'Lord Mellon, I beg your pardon, I had quite forgot you were still here,' she said without guile.

'I think you are very refreshing for my odiously overblown opinion of myself,' he said with a quiet laugh. Mariah thought there was concern in his eyes as he glanced toward her papa. 'Perhaps it would be better if I called again, Miss Fox, when affairs here have been talked over and resolved?'

'Not at all, your lordship,' Jerome said. 'I am not so enfeebled by my disappointment that I might not offer you a glass of wine. Do we have any wine, Mariah?'

'A glass of wine would be most pleasant on another occasion, sir, but I must return to Grosvenor Square; I fear my mama will by now have recovered her sensibility from a shock she received earlier and be in need of my presence,' he said.

'That is very conscientious of you, my lord.' Jerome smiled.

'Alas, I fear I have been the cause of some of her distress, and she will more than likely ring a peal about my ears.'

105

'Mariah was to accompany Mr Sharp to one of his mechanics' classes tomorrow,' Jerome said to no one in particular. He ran a hand over some pamphlets on the edge of his table, and Mariah held her breath. She could always tell when her papa was going to act out of character by his actions more than his words. His apparent absorption in the publications indicated that some outlandish idea was struggling to rise to the surface of his crowded intellect, and it might be given voice at any time. Even, perhaps, while his lordship was still in the room.

'I think Lord Mellon must be about his business, Papa,' she said, trying, and almost succeeding, in suppressing the panic that made her dress feel too tight. She teased the lace around her neckline with her fingers. Her skin was hot and a little clammy. What could he have in mind? 'We should not detain him further.'

'Of course not, my dear; but as I was saying, tomorrow you were to go out with Mr Sharp,' he said, smiling broadly at them. 'Tomorrow, you are now at liberty should Lord Mellon wish to take you driving.'

Mariah paled. This was worse than anything she might have imagined. 'Papa?' she asked in a faint voice nothing like her usual confident tones. 'Papa, I do not go driving.'

'And what a great pity that is,' Jerome said. 'You would enjoy the experience. I imagine the sensation of speed when travelling in an open rig with the breeze lifting your hair would be most exhilarating. Is it not, my lord?'

'Indeed it is, sir. And with your permission, I would be delighted to take Miss Fox driving. Shall we say eleven, Miss Fox?'

Mariah knew she had been manipulated, but she did not know why. Oh, certainly Lord Mellon was playing the kind of flirtatious games he no doubt enjoyed as second nature; but what game was her papa engaged in, and why did it make her feel as if she stood on a sandy slope rather than solid floor-boards? She realised the silence in the room was lengthening and it was up to her to answer.

'I have not been driven in an open carriage,' she said at last. 'I think I would like to try the experience at least once.'

She saw Mellon's lips twitch a little when she made this proper little speech, but he suppressed his mirth and made her a punctilious bow. 'Till eleven,' he said, and within minutes was gone from the house.

6

Mariah sat at her mirror while Tilly drew a brush through her hair. The girl was excited and chattered unceasingly.

'Letty says as how the family is divided over Lady Mellon's wish to go and live in Spain, and more particularly about her plan to take Lady Daisy with her when she goes. Lady Daisy has only been included in the plan since the day a Mr Brent slammed out of the house, breaking a marble urn on his way,' she burbled happily, teasing Mariah's hair into a style they both realised emulated Lady Daisy's more than a little. Mariah squeaked as the brush stuck in her blonde tresses and Tilly had to concentrate while she untangled it.

'Sorry, miss, your hair be so thick and all. Anyways, the household is real glad Lord Mellon ain't going because they reckon he's a good master, and if he could just find a nice lady and set up his nursery then life would be near enough perfect,' she said, once the tangles she'd made in Mariah's hair were smoothed and her mind could swerve back to the endless interest of a titled family and its goings-on. 'Do you know, miss, he sent Letty down to the kitchen to wait for him?' she asked.

'Yes, I was there, Tilly. I suppose it must be considered unusual.'

'Letty reckons it's because his lordship knew she'd never find her way back to Grosvenor Square on her own. She's just arrived up from the Mellons' country seat, two days ago.'

She threaded some amber coloured-ribbon through the curls she'd managed to create from Mariah's hair, and stood back to survey her handiwork in the mirror. The eyes of mistress and maid met, and Mariah could tell Tilly was hoping her drive with Lord Mellon would lead to the need for more such sessions. The girl's young face was alive. Lord Mellon was the most exciting thing to have ever happened in Redde Place.

'Perhaps we shouldn't gossip about Lord Mellon and his relatives,' Mariah said gently, although she would have loved to know why Mr Brent needed to slam out of the house. He seemed much too indolent to slam anywhere.

'It's not a bad thing, Miss, for Letty to say she appreciated his consideration in not sending her back on her own,' Tilly said, but she dropped her eyes and Mariah felt a pang of guilt.

'I'm sorry, Tilly, but this won't come to anything, you know. Lord Mellon has not thought through his intentions with any care . . . ' she said, but the words dried in her throat. Had Lord Mellon invited Letty to wait so that she wouldn't get lost? Or had he hoped the girl would drop the kind of hints she had in Mariah's kitchen?

'Papa has asked Lord Mellon to take me driving,' she said, and saw the bewilderment in Tilly's eyes. 'He is simply acting to oblige him.'

'Yes, miss.' Tilly lifted the new bonnet which they had both decided was the only headwear Mariah possessed fit to be seen in an open carriage. She balanced it on her fingers and turned it around. Mariah had watched in some surprise earlier while Tilly ripped off the green bands of ribbon that had matched her dress yesterday, and replaced them with amber ones from the same roll as those she had threaded through Mariah's hair. Tilly's quick fingers had done a beautiful job. Mariah could almost believe it was a different hat.

'Letty did say that the countess has had six evening soy-rays, two garden lunches, and a ball this season already, but that the earl rarely attends for more than half an hour and only danced with his sister and his married cousin at the ball. The older staff members think he's not in any hurry to assume all the duties of being the earl. He was the second son, you know, Miss Mariah.'

'Lord Mellon did mention an older

brother yesterday but I had thought he died in childhood,' Mariah said, remembering the earl's whispered confidence about their grandmother.

'Oh no, miss. A sword wound, it was. Went bad,' Tilly said darkly. 'Anyways, the countess is desperate to get the new earl married, and she — ' The girl drew breath before saying in obvious enjoyment: ' — Letty says, she throws things.' Tilly imparted this information with relish, disobeying Mariah's injunction to cease her gossip. 'Afterwards, when the guests have gone. And Lord Mellon hasn't singled out any young lady for his particular attention, or to go driving in his curricle,' she concluded in triumph. Mariah knew Tilly was making sure she realised how singular the honour bestowed on her was.

'I have seen her throw things,' Mariah said, recalling the lady's frightening surge of pique swelling into anger. She stood up and smiled at Tilly. 'You have made me look entirely presentable, Tilly.'

'Thank you, miss. I have two sisters what are ladies' maids and they've given me hints and suggestions. Our mum is a seamstress, too, so I've always known how to use a needle.' Tilly tugged the cotton of Mariah's walking dress to help it fall freely. 'You do suit that brown stripe, miss. The earl may be obligating Mr Fox, but it ain't going to be no hardship for him,' she concluded.

★　★　★

Mariah heard Tilly close the house door behind her twenty minutes later. The Earl of Mellon had not kept her waiting, but had arrived on the doorstep to peal the bell at ten minutes before the hour. She stepped across the pavement, narrower than the pavements in Grosvenor Square, and smiled shyly at her host. Whatever the depths of her anger and mortification yesterday, there could be no young woman alive who wouldn't be excited by the prospect of climbing into such an elegant vehicle as the earl had pulled up.

'I am pleased to see you smile, Miss Fox,' he said, and handed her into the high seat upholstered in maroon leather. He took his place beside her and his groom tossed the reins to him before clambering up behind. The earl set his equipage in motion and Mariah held her breath.

'It is not necessary to be so very nervous, Miss Fox. I am reckoned to have driving skills second to none,' the earl said, and she heard the gentle mockery designed to help her relax and enjoy the outing.

'You do not practise any false modesty, my lord,' she said. 'Indeed, I am impressed by the niceness of judgement with which you avoided that coal cart.'

'I think you mean I should not have been so close to the cart in the first place,' he replied, and was silent for a couple of moments while he extricated them from the press of delivery vehicles and slower carriages carrying ladies around town on their morning visits. There would be much of that kind of traffic until they arrived at the gates of Hyde Park and won through to the calmer rides. 'And you would not be wrong,' he added at last. 'I am captivated by the way new experiences light up your face with interest.'

'My lord,' Mariah protested, 'I am here to oblige my papa. You are here to oblige my papa. It is not required that you should flirt with me as if I were one of the eligible young ladies Lady Mellon has picked out for your consideration.' She felt the horses check, and looking sideways, saw that the earl's fingers were gripping the reins tightly. Perhaps she should not have spoken so, but she was bewildered by his determined assault on her sensibilities.

'My mama has torn up her list of eligible young ladies,' the earl said with a touch of asperity, 'and not before time.' He concentrated on his team, but when they were moving smoothly once more, Mariah felt his dark brown gaze slide sideways to fix her with its intensity. She had given offence. Should she apologise?

'I would not wish there to be any misunderstanding between us, your lordship,' she ventured. 'I am not looking for a husband, as I have dedicated myself to my work at the present time.'

'I am not averse to the spread of literacy, Miss Fox. Indeed, I think the country would benefit from a workforce able to read simple instructions.'

'But . . . ?'

'There is a 'but',' he said, and took a deep breath. 'It is a selfish thing, too, and I have asked myself why I think the way I do several times since I lifted you off your feet,' he replied. 'It is that I do wish to marry you; and, as my mother pointed out, the position of Countess of Mellon is an onerous one.'

'Many titled ladies do nothing except entertain themselves,' she said.

'That's true, too, but it has not been the way my mama filled the role, and I find I am conservative enough to wish for a lady who would have a sense of duty and fill the role creditably,' he added. 'Of course, it may be that you are a person with sufficient energies to fulfil that role, and also to teach and provide me with an heir.'

'You are altogether too frank for my liking, Lord Mellon.' Mariah shifted uneasily.

'Come, come, Miss Fox. When Mr Sharp proposed, did he talk about the beating of his heart? Has he snatched kisses when Mr Fox had his head bowed over a difficult work?' Mariah heard the challenge he was throwing to her. 'Has he felt your warm young body melt against him when he whispers in your ear?'

'I did not 'melt against' you, your lordship. That, at least, is all down to your imagination,' she protested. 'I must be clear to you that Peter Sharp has not been making love to me among the books and papers in Redde Place.'

'It is all too clear. Mr Sharp believed you would fall into his arms when your papa pressed you to accept him, or became enfeebled and left you in need of another home,' he said.

'This is nonsense, my lord. I do not think my papa would press me to accept the hand of a man I did not love,' Mariah said.

'Is this truly so, Miss Fox? Your papa is a rather unworldly gentleman, and had I not appeared in your life, I fear he had not thought beyond Peter Sharp as a match for you. I think you would do well to consider my suit very carefully. Think how much easier it would be for you to access premises and funds for teaching as the Countess of Mellon.'

'But you have said that your wife must act as a consort dedicated to your needs.'

'So she must, but at the same time there will be other young teachers whose careers she could further and progress,' he said with inexorable logic.

'It is surely of more concern that teaching should happen than that it should be accomplished by one individual?'

'I love teaching,' she said simply.

'Then is it not your duty to take advantage of every opportunity presented to you to advance the cause?' he asked.

'By marrying where there is no love, nor even any association?' she countered. 'Are you suggesting I should sacrifice myself for this cause?'

'From my observations of your demeanour when dealing with Mr Sharp and with your delightful, if vague, father, I think you already are sacrificing yourself. Marriage to me would not amount to such depressing martyrdom.'

'You *do* have an odiously inflated opinion of yourself.' She threw his words of the previous afternoon back at him.

For the first time, she began to understand why a man like Lord

Mellon might want to marry Mariah Fox, schoolteacher. He did not want a woman as the love of his life. He wanted a slave to relieve him of the burden of dealing with the poor on his estates and the pensioners. He wanted a reliable, boring helpmeet to stay at home and deal with things while he went to London and entertained his mistress. Did he keep a mistress?

'And this is what you wished to tell me yesterday before we discovered Peter Sharp with my papa,' she said coldly. 'That your mama has worked hard in the family's service for many years, and now deserves to retire to Spain to spend her declining years in the sunshine of her birth country.'

'Yes, it is. It is so very refreshing, Miss Fox, to deal with a woman whose brain grasps fact and does not confuse the essential business nature of marriage with the romantic fallacies of the circulating libraries.'

'You are well-read in romances, then, your lordship?'

'No, but Daisy is,' he said, and guided the curricle through the gates of the park. 'She insists on recounting them to me in tedious detail. What do you say to my proposal?'

'Which proposal, your lordship? That we should make a turn around the park and go straight back to Redde Place?' she snapped.

Suddenly, Mariah realised she did want romance. It startled her to learn it because she had always assumed she would find enough satisfaction contracting a marriage after a quiet, comfortable courtship. Now, sitting in this gorgeous carriage with one of London's most eligible bachelors, she knew differently.

She did not want to become any kind of sacrificial victim. If the Earl of Mellon was finding his life uncomfortably constrained by family responsibilities while he only had a mama and a sister, both in rude health, then what kind of husband would he make?

'Why, Miss Fox, is this a show of

temperament? I merely go on as I thought you would wish,' he protested mildly. 'You did tell Mr Sharp that you were well able to think when he made such an eloquent case for the lack of reasoning and logic in the brain of the female and its inability to see consequences.'

'My lord, I have already told you that I do not wish to marry you. I think you should rescue your mama's list from her bin and — '

'I should not dream of interrupting a lady in ordinary circumstances, Miss Fox, but it is impossible to rescue the list. She tossed it into the fire. She and Anna, her companion, are now deep in producing other lists: lists of the necessities a countess would take with her on an extended visit to Spain,' the earl said, and eased the curricle to a walk.

Mariah caught sight of other carriages moving slowly around the park, and soon one or two horsemen appeared alongside them. The earl seemed in no hurry to disengage from their conversation.

'Your lordship, is it not the case that we may be overheard?' Mariah said, as calmly as she could. She might not be a member of the *ton*, but she understood how gossip got its fatal grip. Gossip fed through the meshes between one layer of society and the others. She was jealous of her reputation in the narrow world of teaching. Any hint of scandal concerning herself and an aristocrat could cost her dearly when she next appeared before a panel of ladies allocating funds.

'I think you are right; we may be overheard. If I desist from pursuing my suit at present, will you consent to accept the invitation my mama has entrusted me to deliver to you? It is for a card party, and it includes your papa,' he said, and drew the curricle to a stand.

Mariah heard a horse, recognised Mr Brent as one of the horsemen alongside them, and remembered her worry that he might send snippets of gossip to the newspapers. She made a snap decision. No doubt it could be changed later when her papa refused to attend.

'Yes. We will come. Please thank the countess for me.'

Tobias acknowledged her acquiescence with a slight bow, and, hooding his eyes, turned his attention to Brent and his riding companion, Sir Lucas Wellwood. If John was a dear friend, Wellwood was not. He was renowned for his malicious mischief-making and uncertain temper. John would not usually seek out his company, Tobias knew.

'Toby,' John said, and turned immediately to his companion. 'And the delightful Miss Fox. Do I find you in good spirits, ma'am?' John sat easily in the saddle for such a big man, and his hired horse seemed happy to stand. Tobias thought his friend was more cheerful than he had been of late, and genuinely pleased to find Miss Fox taking the air where he might converse with her. Tobias bristled. What business did Brent have in finding Mariah Fox's company congenial?

'You are abroad early, John,' he said, in an attempt to steer his friend's attention away from Mariah. 'And with company for the ride, too,' he added, not wishing to seem lacking in good manners, although he had no desire to devote any time to Lucas Wellwood.

'Your lordship,' Wellwood said. He made a small bow. Tobias acknowledged the courtesy. He wondered what Miss Fox would make of the dark-skinned fellow whose eyes were slits of murky disdain. He was small by comparison with Tobias and John, but that didn't cause such an impression when he was astride a large bay gelding. He had removed his hat and now sat waiting to be offered an introduction to Tobias's driving companion.

'Sir Lucas,' he said, because he couldn't see any way of avoiding it, 'may I introduce Miss Mariah Fox, who is a protégée of my mama's.' He felt the protégée stiffen at his side, and offered up a silent prayer that she didn't think being an educationalist meant she also had to adhere to the truth. The reality of their relationship so far would provide Lucas with more than enough material to begin a campaign to malign her with the *ton*. Mariah's silence emboldened him to turn his head and send her a speaking glance. Her blue eyes sparkled as always, but whether with mischief or anger, he could not discern. 'Miss Fox, Sir Lucas Wellwood of Doveton.'

He watched with relief as Mariah inclined her head. She was wearing a fetching bonnet with elegant amber ribbons, and it set off her ash-blonde hair to perfection. The desire to tell her so surprised him, and he caught the edge of his tongue with his teeth, preventing the words slipping through.

'A protégée?' Lucas queried in his nasal voice. 'The estimable countess Constanzia has many talents and fields of interest, Miss Fox. Which of them involves you to the extent that she has noticed your abilities and shown her admiration?'

'Miss Fox is an educationalist, Wellwood, and daughter of Jerome Fox,' Tobias said before Mariah could reply.

If Wellwood noticed his hurry to get hold of the conversation and keep the lady quiet, he did not give himself away, but came back smartly with a history of Jerome's family.

'I think you must be one of the Foxes from Hampshire then, ma'am,' he said. 'Your papa's father would be the younger son of Sir Trent Fox, and great-grandson of Lady Isabella Burbage.'

'Gawd, Wellwood,' John said. 'Is there no one whose lineage you can't describe to the smallest degree? Miss Fox hasn't come out this morning to converse about things she already knows. Have you, ma'am?'

'It didn't seem as if I were to converse at all,' Mariah said, sweetening the waspish remark with a smile that showed beautiful white teeth. 'I believe there is a peerage somewhere in the last century, Sir Lucas, but my papa does not reflect on such things. His interests are all to do with how a man goes on in his own life.'

'And yet here is his daughter driving in the park with a belted earl,' Wellwood riposted, and Tobias clenched the reins. How dare the man?

'Not all of us spend our leisure hours steeped in the peerage,' John said. 'As I well know, family connection dilutes in very few generations.'

'Lord Mellon does have an earldom, Sir Lucas, but my papa has not held that against him, and was pleased to allow me to accompany him this morning,' Mariah said, and Tobias knew the day could hardly become more blighted. Why didn't the chit just tell Wellwood he had made her an unconventional offer of marriage, and then open warfare could be declared? However, Wellwood surprised him by laughing.

'Ma'am, you have our measure. It was rude of me to make such comparisons. I hope you will permit me the opportunity to redeem myself when we meet next,' Wellwood said, and prepared to set his beast in motion. 'Brent?'

'I'll catch you up, Wellwood,' John Brent said, and they all watched as the horse pulled away, taking the baronet out of earshot.

'I am not likely to meet him again, Lord Mellon. I do wish you would stop frowning as if I had related the whole of our history to him,' Mariah said, and Tobias gathered his wits. John remained with them; and, following their recent words about his mama's hopes for his early marriage, would be sure to invest anything Mariah said with romantic overtones.

'What is the whole of your history, Miss Fox?' John Brent asked as casually as he could, but Mariah turned a dazzling smile toward him.

'You have been present at almost all

of it, Mr Brent,' she said. 'Most of the rest of it has been shared by tripping maidservants, my papa, and his help-meet Peter Sharp. As you will assess, nothing is hidden and all is proper, even boring, for anyone of a romantic disposition.'

Tobias seethed with impotence. Miss Fox could not have handed John Brent a clearer indication that nothing was open, proper, or boring if she had hired a town crier to proclaim it at the village cross.

7

Mariah tugged the ribbons on her precious new bonnet viciously, until she felt them part and shred beneath her fingers. With no thought for its safe landing, she tossed the hat across the room. It dislodged a pile of papers onto the floor and tumbled after them.

How dare he? She fumed inwardly. How dare he make me such an insulting offer and why? Why me? She paced the floor of her bedroom and came to a standstill in front of the mirror. Only two hours ago, she and Tilly had each indulged ridiculous fancies here. As if conjured by her riotous thoughts, Tilly entered.

'I did knock, miss, but . . . ' The girl let out a squeal of dismay. 'Why, miss, you've thrown that lovely bonnet, and now look.' Tilly dashed across the room and lifted the hat. It had a dent in it and some of the straw looked torn.

'There must have been a book in that pile of papers,' Mariah said.

'You threw it, miss,' Tilly said, but the outrage in her tone changed to sympathy when she caught sight of her young mistress's face. 'Didn't you enjoy the drive, miss?'

'The drive was full of interest, and Lord Mellon's curricle is the last word in style and speed and everything a society lady might wish her beau to be seen driving,' Mariah said generously, but Tilly did not appear fooled. The girl watched her, waiting for her to explain why such splendour meant she had to throw her bonnet across the room. 'Lord Mellon has asked Papa and me to an evening party being held at Mellon House on Sunday,' she said.

'And you are afraid the master will turn it down as he always does,' Tilly said, understanding flooding her features.

'No, he has accepted,' Mariah said. 'He came out to view the equipage when he saw our return from his window. Lord Mellon took the chance to tell him about the invitation and he was exceeding glad to accept.' Mariah sank onto a chair. She felt exhausted by the strain of trying to work out what kind of spell Mellon had cast over her papa. She had never known him to accept a society invitation. If there had been a few months when she was younger and that irritated her, she was long past that.

Her life had purpose and meaning. She might be dependent, as she had hinted to Lady Daisy, but she could secure work and board with her teaching and reputation very easily. She did not need to hang on Mellon's every word, or hope that he would declare himself among the ferns of his mama's conservatory. Drat it all! The man had already declared himself and was now trying to secure her agreement.

'A gentleman does not send his mama, what is a countess, to call on a lady if he intends to make her his mistress,' Tilly said quietly. She stroked the bonnet with her work-worn hands and Mariah followed their sweeps. Given half a chance, she would make a good lady's maid with her skills and her even temperament. 'A gentleman like Lord Mellon — '

'He does not wish to make me his mistress,' Mariah said, interrupting Tilly. 'He has asked me to be his wife.'

Tilly's hands stilled and the dangling ribbons moved in the breeze from the open window. She lifted her head and gazed into Mariah's eyes. Mariah felt hot tears sliding down her cheeks.

'But, miss,' Tilly said gently, 'what could be better?'

'Love, perhaps, such as my mama must have felt for Papa. He wants to marry me in order to release his mother from the constraints of being Countess of Mellon. He thinks I don't need to be wooed because I am of strong intellect,' Mariah said, and dashed the tears from her cheeks. How could she be so faint-hearted?

'Does he?' Tilly said. 'Not everyone thinks as you and your papa do. I expect Lord Mellon *does* think only ladies in the upper classes have feelings.'

'I think it's time Lord Mellon learned a lesson in the gentler arts, Tilly,' Mariah said, and her helpmeet chuckled. 'But there is a practical problem because I do not have any clothes suitable for moving among the people I will meet at Mellon House.'

'We have that trunk in the attic, miss, with your late mama's clothes. The fashions won't do, but I can alter and cut down and use the material,' Tilly said. 'My sister is visiting our aunt for two days and she would come and help.'

Mariah stood up and crossed to her mirror to remove her shawl. Tilly lingered in the background, clearly wanting to say something else.

'When you become countess, miss, will there be places for Cook and me?' she asked, and Mariah heard the longing in her voice as well as another emotion. In the mirror she glanced at the top of Tilly's bent head. It was ambition. Tilly had no intention of remaining a maid of all work. She was determined to move on and was not afraid of asking for what she wanted.

A voice of mellow Somerset vowels sounded in her head. 'Is it not your duty to take advantage of every opportunity offered to you to advance the cause?' he had asked her.

Duty, Mariah thought, *I've lived the most dutiful life it's possible to conceive. I don't want him to take me because of that. If he takes me as his countess, I want to be loved, too. If Tilly can aim for the stars, why can't I? What am I being so feeble over? I will make the earl fall in love with me; and if I like that new version of Tobias Mellon, why, I may think again about my refusal. On the other hand, I cannot see myself simply abandoning worthwhile work in order to make an earl's life even easier than it is already.*

She wound a lock of hair around her finger and smiled at her reflection. It would be a triumph to teach the man a lesson. He should not assume the whole world was ready to fall into line with his requests. The smile broadened. Yes, making Tobias Mellon lovelorn would make her future refusals much sweeter.

The evening party is a very good place to begin my campaign, I think. But I need to dazzle so that he does not even glance at the other females there. Tilly and I have work to do.

* * *

'Mariah,' Jerome said testily as he picked his way around the ancient trunk she had hauled out onto the landing, 'do you and Tilly have to create so much confusion?'

'Papa, I have no clothes suitable for wearing to an evening party. Had we not received the countess's invitation, then I would not need to be rooting

138

among Mama's dresses.' She held up a gown of white silk with an overdress of net. It had been stored well and the material had not yellowed.

'Stop this nonsense at once,' Jerome said, and both mistress and maid turned astonished eyes to him. Mariah thought she had only ever heard him speak so when confronted by bullying masters in the streets. Tilly had possibly never heard him raise his voice.

'Of course, sir, but I must have something to wear. We will take the trunk into my room,' Mariah offered quietly.

'No. Send it back to the attic, Tilly!'

'Yes sir,' the maid said and dropped a swift curtsy as she went in search of Cook to assist her.

'I am most remiss as a parent, Mariah, but even I realise that your changed status requires funds,' Jerome said.

'Changed status? What do you mean by that, Papa? I had no intended husband yesterday and I still have none today,' Mariah said as calmly as she could.

Jerome scratched his ear and stood as if lost in thought for a moment or two. 'That's as may be, but we *do* have an earl and his mother dropping in to see us and to take you out to fashionable haunts. Your education is already a handicap when it comes to finding a husband, and I would not have your clothes single you out for further adverse comment.'

'I am not searching for a husband,' Mariah protested. *It will make my mischievous pursuit of the earl a lot more dangerous if Papa is determined to regard him as a suitor*, she thought. *I hope I have not started another impetuous plan that will get me into trouble.* 'You have never alluded to this before yesterday, Papa. Why should you begin now? Do we not go on tolerably well together?'

'Of course, but I see from the way Peter Sharp reacted that I have been too sanguine. I will not live forever, my darling girl, and I would not wish your light to be eclipsed by someone like him who recognises what an exceptional brain you have and wants to use it for his own advancement. No.' He held up a hand when Mariah would have interrupted him. 'No, do not argue. If the earl does not come up to the mark, then at least you will have had a taste of society and sophistication. Who knows, you may meet other wealthy men, or indeed a female benefactress, who will provide funds to advance your ideas. I have sent for Mr Routledge and I expect him to call later this morning. He will bring money with him, and he has been instructed to arrange with one of the warehouses that you may make more expensive purchases and send the accounts to him for settlement.'

Mariah moved ahead of her father down the stairs and into the morning room. Her thoughts were in confusion. Papa had never before suggested that she should spend large sums of money on her wardrobe, and she had been content with that. Sturdy boots and warm outerwear were necessities for going out to teach in the unheated chapel halls they used, particularly during the colder months, but dresses bought from a warehouse had never been a priority when she could make them herself.

'Your man of business is making a personal call?' she asked while she tried to make sense of her father's actions. Excitement caught the breath in her throat and made her voice a little husky. She would be able to choose a variety of fabrics. She would be able to handle silk and satin and velvet and make choices. Wearing fashionable garments would certainly help Tobias to see her as a woman and not simply as a solution.

'Mariah, I have money set aside for your marriage, you know. I am not able to settle very much on you, and if you marry Lord Mellon that amount will seem like a drop in the Thames, but there is something,' Jerome said, as he sank into his favourite chair.

Mariah thought how easily exertion made her papa seek a chair recently. 'Are you quite well, Papa?' she asked.

'Of course, my dear. Just old age beginning to reach my knees,' he replied and smiled. Mariah returned his smile, but she knew a nagging worry that she had not felt before.

'Besides, I find it pains me to see your mother's clothes even after all this time.'

'I beg your pardon, Papa. It was thoughtless of me.' Mariah was full of contrition. She had not thought how the sight of her mama's clothes would affect him. Would a husband continue to feel such loss after twenty years, if he had taken his wife out of duty?

The doorbell pealed in the hall, and Mariah went to answer because she could hear Tilly and cook struggling with the heavy trunk upstairs. As she peeked through the side-light, she saw the Mellons' town coach drawn up in front of the house. Daisy's bright head was visible through one of its windows.

⋆   ⋆   ⋆

Mariah listened to Daisy's flow of chatter as they made a stately progress through the streets toward the girl's favourite modiste. Mademoiselle Juliette would be enchanted by Mariah's fair skin and luxuriant hair, and would know exactly how to dress her for the evening party and, should Mariah wish it, for any number of activities.

Daisy had clearly been sent by her brother to ensure Mariah had a suitable outfit for the evening party, but she did not trouble herself worrying about that. It was such a relief to have sympathetic company when entering the daunting world of the professional dressmaker for the first time. Mariah was suddenly very keen indeed to pursue the best she and Tilly could make of her appearance. It was essential, if she was to cause the earl to fall in love with her, to compete in all respects with the pampered girls of the *haut ton*.

They had been in the salon for nearly an hour. Mariah had chosen two evening dresses and two morning gowns from an array of lovely garments paraded before her. She was considering a beautiful floor-length cloak made from Chinese silk when a nasal twang cut into the buzz of conversation.

'Oh no,' Daisy murmured, as she fingered the length of rose-coloured silk Mademoiselle felt sure would enhance the olive tones the girl inherited from her mama. 'Amarinta Wellwood.'

Mariah did not turn her head, but noticed Mademoiselle frowned a little when she heard the distinctive voice, and turned away with a curtsy to attend to her newly-arrived customer.

'Is Miss Wellwood related to a gentleman your brother introduced me to this morning?' Mariah asked. 'Sir Lucas Wellwood?'

'Toby introduced you to that man! I can hardly credit it, Miss Fox. He must have been pushed into a corner,' she said. She handed the bale of silk to one of the modiste's assistants and stood up. 'I am afraid I will have to speak to Amarinta. She is a particular pet of Mama's.'

They passed through the drapes of the small area in which they had been viewing gowns, and crossed the salon. Mademoiselle and the new arrival stood a little apart. Mademoiselle had her hand on an open ledger and Mariah wondered if the newcomer was there to collect a gown. She studied her.

The girl was beautiful. Her hair was cut at the front to allow ringlets of thick, lustrous chestnut to escape from her bonnet and frame a small face of near-ivory complexion. No freckles marred her skin and her eyes gleamed emerald. Mariah thought the girl's lips hinted at cruelty, but instantly chided herself for the wayward thought. How could she make such a judgement about anyone without evidence?

'Amarinta,' Daisy gushed, and Mariah started. The girl had been affable and entertaining, but her manner had also been entirely natural. Why did Amarinta draw such a society voice from her? Mariah paid more attention to the exchange than she might have done. 'Amarinta,' 'Daisy said again, 'how delightful to meet you, and unexpected.'

'I saw the carriage waiting, Daisy, and knew you were most likely to be here,' Amarinta said, and turned her head to cast those emerald eyes, now full of disdain, over Mariah. 'Does your maid have to stand so close?'

Daisy's face fired but Mariah suppressed a desire to giggle. She glanced at the elderly Frenchwoman who was still studying her ledger, and whose face had also changed colour at Amarinta's remarks. Was this an example of what she might expect to encounter at Mellon House on Sunday evening? she wondered. Mariah knew enough about the complicated mores of her betters to understand that she should not address Miss Wellwood before being introduced.

So she spoke.

'Goodness, Miss Wellwood,' she said, 'I am not well enough presented to be Daisy's maid. But if you thought so, then I live in hopes of Mademoiselle Juliette being able to transform me into someone presentable enough.'

'Into a lady's maid!' Amarinta said. The words spilled from her and Mariah wondered how she had thought the girl beautiful. Venom twisted her features and made her figure rigid.

'I think not. Servility has been educated out of me,' Mariah said, and with a quiet thank-you to Mademoiselle, she left the shop.

On the pavement, she stopped to wait for Daisy and caught sight of *that man*, as Daisy had described Sir Lucas Wellwood, leaning against the railings in front. He twirled a cane with one hand. An assistant came from the salon and deposited several parcels in the Mellons' carriage. The bustle caused Wellwood to turn, and when he saw

Mariah his eyes flashed with some emotion she could not interpret. It was shuttered in an instant and he strolled across the space between them.

'Good afternoon, Miss Fox,' he said, and Mariah inclined her head in response. For all her brave words to his sister, she had been upset by the encounter and could not find her voice at once.

'Have you been shopping with Lady Mellon, *your benefactress?*' he asked, and inserted enough sarcasm for Mariah to understand he did not for one moment believe Lord Mellon's claim.

'Not with Lady Mellon but with Lady Daisy,' Mariah said mildly. 'She has been offering me invaluable advice about my wardrobe.'

'Then we may expect to see you more in society than has been the case?' the Baronet asked.

'My father has decided to accept one or two invitations, Sir Lucas.' Mariah offered no further intelligence.

'Mariah,' Daisy said behind her, bustling out of the shop and across the flagged entrance, 'James is waiting. Sir Lucas,' she added and dipped her head. Mariah saw James; the coachman, on the box, and one of the grooms ready with a step to assist the ladies into the carriage.

'Lady Daisy,' Wellwood said, and offered a polite bow. Mariah was struck by the way his eyes narrowed to slits as he allowed his gaze to rake Lady Daisy's figure in a frankly insolent manner. 'I understand you are steering Miss Fox's entry into society.'

'Miss Fox does not need me to steer her anywhere, except into the carriage which I must return to Grosvenor Square in order that my mama may not be kept waiting,' she replied briskly. 'Even spoiled daughters will have their privileges removed should they abuse them too often.'

'Who has spoken to you in such a cruel fashion, Lady Daisy?' Wellwood asked, keeping his position on the pavement between the ladies and the carriage. 'Surely you are able to manipulate that brother of yours? He must be a very hardened soldier if he does not respond to the beauty of his sister.'

'Your own sister awaits you inside,' Daisy said, stepping nimbly around him and catching Mariah's arm as she moved. 'She seemed a little distrait when I left her.'

* * *

Mariah said nothing as the vehicle drew away and manoeuvred into the traffic. Daisy was agitated and she concluded that an argument of sorts had taken place between her and her *mama's pet*, Amarinta. They travelled a mile or so in silence before she spoke.

'I do trust, Daisy, that you have not quarrelled with Miss Wellwood on my behalf,' she said, making a guess at the cause of her obvious discomfiture. 'I will only be in your lives for a very short time and it would not be good to lose a long-standing friend over a supposed insult.'

'It was an *actual* insult, Mariah. She looks like an angel and has the mind of a rat such as one would find in the midden. I have witnessed her words bring dear ladies to tears and send young men out of the room to vent their frustration on some unfortunate servant.'

'But never in your mama's presence?' Mariah said quietly.

'As you say,' the girl agreed, waving a hand gloved in palest grey kid around. 'I would be embarrassed to continue counting her as a friend. We used to exchange the frothiest of girlish confidences in letters tied up with red ribbon.' Daisy's eyes widened as if in disbelief that such a thing could be true. 'But I will never call her sister again.'

Mariah was in a quandary. She knew from her drive with the earl that Lady Mellon considered Miss Wellwood to be an eligible bride for her son. His lordship, however, had no intention of accommodating her on this point at the present time as he had asked — no, told — Mariah he intended to marry *her*. How far did Daisy enter into the earl's confidence?

'You need not tell me how things stand between you and Toby, Mariah, but I know he would never marry Amarinta Wellwood. Besides, I overheard Mademoiselle's greeting to her as I went into the main salon. I think the Wellwood finances may be in dire straits. Mama would not mind that.' Daisy's complexion coloured a little but Mariah could see she had decided to finish her outburst. 'She herself comes from a noble but impoverished line. No, the problem would be welcoming Lucas into the family when Mama was told of his true nature.'

'His true nature?' Mariah asked before she could stop herself.

'It is known that several persons have died unexpectedly on his estate. He has an uncontrollable temper when thwarted,' Daisy said. 'I think her man of business, at least, would ensure this was made known to my mama were there any question of nuptials.'

'Has your brother told you this?'

'Goodness, no. I listen to the servants' chatter and actively encourage my maid to gossip. I wish to try my hand at writing books, you know. Where would I find anything interesting to write about among my mama's circle of acquaintance?'

Mariah sank back into the cushions. If she were of an imaginative nature, she felt she'd encountered enough of interest in the last week to write a three-volume romance. Daisy's standards of outrageousness must be very high.

8

Mariah's eye was drawn to Tobias as soon as she crossed the threshold of Grosvenor Square on Sunday evening. He stood at the head of the staircase with his mama and Daisy welcoming their guests. She gripped the pearl-handled fan her papa had presented her with before they left Redde Place, and, noticing how anxious Jerome was, fussed a little over him.

It was already dark enough for candles and some lamps to have been lit, and the house sparkled. Light reflected off mirrors and sconces. It fractured into myriad flashes as it hit the crystals of the elegant chandeliers. Mariah gave up her new silk cloak to the young footman who had attended the drawing room party on Thursday morning.

'Why, it's Alfred, isn't it?' she said in

155

her clear contralto, remembering the name the butler had used. The young man looked startled but offered her a shy smile as he threw her cloak over his arm and waited for Jerome to divest his coat.

'Thank you,' Jerome said, and the footman's expression changed into one of puzzlement. They climbed the long stair to the landing where their hosts awaited them.

'Good evening, Miss Fox,' the earl said when they reached the top of the staircase.

Mariah felt her pulse race as she took in the sheer perfection of his evening clothes. Black wool contrasted with the brilliant white linen of his shirt. He had been freshly shaved and his skin was pink and clean, showing his strong jawline and broad cheekbones. The overall effect was of heightened masculinity such as her papa's book-loving compatriots never achieved.

'Mr Fox,' the earl said and bowed. 'Mama, may I present Miss Fox's papa, the distinguished educationalist Mr Jerome Fox?'

'Good evening, Mr Fox,' the countess said graciously, acknowledging Jerome's bow. 'I believe my dear friend, Miss Ellyton, is an acquaintance of your sister.'

'Why indeed, she is, Lady Mellon. She and her brother are well known to those of us in educationalist circles,' Jerome said, clearly delighted with the small connection.

'They are both here this evening.' The countess looked toward a footman who sprang to her side. 'Take Mr Fox along to the Blue Salon and assist him in finding Mr Ellyton.'

Mariah knew a moment of disappointment. How was she going to begin her campaign to captivate the earl if she was sequestered in a blue salon with her papa and his cronies? There could be no escape, however, as she knew no one else apart from her hosts, who were occupied greeting their guests. She dropped a neat curtsy to the countess before preparing to follow Jerome.

'One moment, Miss Fox,' the earl said. 'I am sure you must be in need of a little refreshment.'

'Tobias, only about half of our guests have arrived as yet. How can you think to abandon me?' the countess protested, but with little heat.

'You have Daisy, who is much more likely to know their names and histories than I,' he said. 'Miss Fox?' He extended an arm and Mariah tucked her hand through it, smiling up into his face.

'How thoughtful of you, sir,' she said, hoping her smile would inform the Earl of Mellon she thought he was the only man in the building.

★   ★   ★

Tobias felt the warmth of Mariah's fingers through the fine wool of his evening coat. The skirts of her new gown brushed his legs as they made their way through the throng into the

158

large drawing room.

'You look lovely tonight, Miss Fox,' he said. 'I am sure I will have to keep you close, lest some fellow tries to steal your attention.'

'If you think that is proper, my lord, then I am sure I have no objection.' Her eyes sparkled with mischief and admiration. Tobias frowned. This was not the behaviour he had come to expect from the young lady. 'Besides, I have met only two other gentlemen of the *ton*, and I cannot think that either would keep me entertained for very long.'

'Wellwood is a man you should avoid at any cost,' he said, quickly working out whom she meant, 'but John Brent is a decent sort.'

'You have acquitted him of sending snippets to *The Times*?' she asked.

'I think your supposition was never proven, ma'am, and you are intent on provoking me.' He accepted a glass of champagne for her when a footman materialised at their sides, and then took one for himself. It had been his intention to introduce her to one or two of his relatives, but the new Miss Fox, gazing adoringly at him and offering empty-headed remarks like any other marriage-market miss, troubled him. Had he been entirely mistaken in her character?

'I am told by Daisy that you had an unfortunate encounter on Friday while shopping with her,' he said. They had crossed the room and stood in the windows looking out onto the gardens. Lanterns had been lit and the grounds made a dramatic backdrop. Other guests fell away to allow the earl and this most favoured young lady the chance to converse.

'It is indeed unfortunate to be mistaken for Lady Daisy's maid. It was even less pleasant to encounter Sir Lucas Wellwood when I had no warning of his presence,' she said calmly, and Tobias was reassured that the girl he wished to marry was still there inside the facade of expensive clothing. 'I did not linger in Mademoiselle Juliette's salon because I knew how mortified I would have been to commit an error such as Miss Wellwood did.'

'Daisy tells me Amarinta Wellwood has a poisonous tongue when those she wishes to impress are out of hearing,' he said. 'You need not take any of the blame for her behaviour to yourself.'

'And yet your mama would have you marry her?' she said, dropping her eyelids and pursing her lips in the manner he saw so many others use. She brought her chin up and set her head on one side. 'You may have to get used to it.'

'I think not. Besides, Mama's enduring hope that I will marry someone, and thus facilitate her escape to Spain, would seem to have been answered without calling on the forbearance of Miss Wellwood,' he said.

'How so, my lord?'

'Why, you and your papa are here this evening, and our extended conversation is being observed by every eye in the room,' he said, and waited for her denial. It did not come.

Mariah knew she should offer him a sharp set-down, but the ability to reply deserted her. Panic welled in her breast. It was all very well to set out to capture the heart of the Earl of Mellon, but it would be no use to her plans to lose her own on the way. She could not for one moment allow her heart to think it would be a good idea to marry this man before she had tested whether he was capable of love. She saw her papa's gentle face explaining why he could not allow her to wear her mama's clothes, and knew that was the kind of marriage she wanted for herself.

She felt the seconds pulsing by and the warmth of the room heat her face. How was she to maintain her *sang-froid*, and her purpose, when her entire being ached for the touch of the earl's hand? When she wanted nothing more than to bask in the warmth of his smile?

'Indeed, my lord,' she said, snapping open her fan. 'I think you are a little presumptuous. While I am grateful that your entry into our lives has dislodged Mr Sharp, I cannot pretend that I have changed my views about marriage.'

'I had thought to send you away the other day with an option to mull over,' he replied mildly. 'I had thought to encourage you to realise that education could be advanced by more than one means.' He stepped away a little and sipped some of his wine.

Mariah fanned herself slowly with her papa's gift while she considered her response to his words. 'Yes, you did, and I would be churlish not to acknowledge it,' she replied eventually. 'However, I cannot say that I would be happy to be buried on your country estates while you pursue *entertainment* elsewhere.'

That caught his attention for his eyes flashed in the swirling lights and he held her gaze. 'Were I married to you, Mariah, I would not bury you any-where, and I would most certainly have no need to pursue *entertainment*. What canker has entered into your brain that you risk my good opinion by referring to things no respectable young woman should have knowledge of?'

She recognised now that she was unskilled in the politics between men and women. It was why she had failed to see what Peter was about. The earl's abrupt use of her name was a sharp warning that she was still an ingénue. She had let her imagination invent mistresses and plots that perhaps did not match the earl's character.

'Do not forget, my lord, that I have spent many hours working among the slum children and have seen things that the young ladies of your acquaintance have not,' she said. 'Nor should you forget that my father has not set any boundaries on what subjects are suitable for my ears. In his opinion all subjects may be discussed equally.'

'I did forget,' he said, briefly discomfited. 'You appear here tonight dressed as well as any of the other young ladies, and you flirt with me as outrageously as only the boldest of them would dare to do. Rash behaviour that made me forget that beneath that conventional exterior lies the woman I wish to make my wife. A woman who would not tolerate any dalliance with a mistress.'

'I would, however, have no redress once your ring was on my finger,' she said and met his gaze with her own. She was treading a path that might tempt her to go too far in taunting him.

'No, you would not. My wife will love, honour, and obey,' he said and then, as if he realised how pompous it sounded, he laughed. 'There will be so much for us both to enjoy while I bring you to fulfil your vows.'

'Your lordship,' a nasal voice said at their sides, and Mariah's colour flared. Had Sir Lucas heard any of the last exchanges? She let her eyes fly to the earl for reassurance and read the warning there. She should be circumspect. 'Your mama said you had been forced from her side by the calls of duty. I can see nothing at all onerous in conversing with such beauty. But you must share Miss Fox, my lord. We bachelors are cruelly deprived by the advantages your position conveys.'

Mariah was caught unawares by a flash of hysteria at the import of the Wellwood's words, and struggled not to laugh. Could he have made it any clearer that he was intervening on behalf of his sister? Perhaps, if Daisy's information was correct, a sister whose marriage was necessary to stave off family ruin.

'G'evening, Wellwood,' the earl drawled, and inclined his head. 'Miss Fox was explaining how she met you and your sister while shopping.'

'She did, and my sister was anxious that I should seek to have a few words with Miss Fox, as she feels she may have caused offence,' Wellwood said. He turned those singular eyes, once more closed almost to slits, on Mariah's face. She shuddered involuntarily. 'My sister is of the impression that her words may have been taken out of context.'

'Context does account for much of

understanding,' Mariah said, concealing her irritation. How could the girl pretend she *may have* caused offence by her words? It had been the sole purpose of her uttering them.

'Then, if the earl will release you, I might explain her meaning more clearly,' Wellwood said. 'Amarinta would have done so herself, but she has had a fall and bruised her face. It made her unwilling to appear in public.'

'I am sorry to learn that, Sir Lucas,' Mariah said. 'How did such a thing occur?' She watched as the baronet shook his head. His lip curled impatiently and he raised an eyebrow, adding a sinister aspect to his dark features. Mariah felt a ripple of unease on behalf of the missing girl. Had she indeed suffered an accident, or had she been chastised by a brother whose debts made her acceptance in Mellon House of the first importance?

'Alas, Wellwood,' the earl said, 'Mama has decreed we will eat an early supper this evening, and Miss Fox has already accepted my offer to escort her.'

'Why, an early supper will be delightful. I have decided not to try my luck at the tables tonight and shall offer my arm to Lady Daisy. We can make up a family party,' Wellwood said, clearly determined not to be thwarted. 'Here she comes.'

They turned to see Daisy walking toward them. John Brent was walking rapidly in the other direction. Mariah thought the colour in Daisy's cheeks a little heightened, but could not ask the girl anything while the men were with them.

Wellwood bowed as Daisy approached, and when he would have spoken, Daisy raised an eyebrow and pre-empted him.

'Sir Lucas,' she said and dropped an infinitesimal curtsy. 'Toby, I am come from Mama. She requires our presence in the Blue Salon. You, too, Mariah. She is most imperious this evening and will not be kept waiting.'

'Sir Lucas, my apologies. It seems your plan may have to wait on another occasion,' the earl said calmly. He extended an arm, and Mariah laid her fingers on his strength. They followed Daisy through the throng, now agog with curiosity, and emerged onto the landing.

They had travelled only a few steps when Daisy turned to them and said quietly, 'I hoped that ploy would work and it did.'

'You, miss, are a minx,' the earl said in fierce tones, but they succeeded only in bringing a smile to Daisy's lips.

'Sir Lucas Wellwood is a reptile and he set off with the sole purpose of separating you from Mariah,' she said. 'He could hardly finish presenting his compliments to Mama before his eyes were scouring the rooms.'

'Daisy, you allow your imagination too free a rein. I do believe we will all be better served should you in fact turn to writing three-volume romances. It will relieve us of the necessity of acting out imaginary dramas for your satisfaction,' the earl said. 'Besides, my love, he was most anxious to take you down to supper. His interest is not fixed on Miss Fox.'

'You would never give him permission to pay me any attention, Toby, would you?' Daisy asked abruptly.

'Has he been annoying you, love?'

'No, but I wish it to stay that way,' Daisy replied.

'Lucas Wellwood has no place in this family,' the earl reassured his sister. Mariah remembered the horrible feeling earlier when the man had cast his strange slit gaze over her. She also remembered the way the baronet had raked Daisy's young form with it on Friday.

He had not thought to modify his behaviour from that of a Bond Street Beau. It was unnerving.

★ ★ ★

They passed quickly through the Blue Salon, where Mariah was amused to see her papa deep in conversation with an

170

elderly couple who must have been the Ellytons and also with Lady Mellon. The room was dotted with other eminent educationalists. Mariah recognised several of her papa's colleagues and at least two ladies who had interviewed her about funds for her classes.

'Papa has not been able to escape your mama this evening as he did when she called,' she said to the earl, 'but I suspect he does not wish to. Did you cause these others to be invited?' she asked, and hurried on at the earl's obvious embarrassment. Men of action rarely enjoyed having their good deeds pointed up, she thought. 'It was very understanding of you and I thank you for it. He is happily engaged.'

'I don't deserve your thanks, Miss Fox,' he said abruptly, and nodded to John Brent who was mingling with the educationalists. 'Now that we have given credence to this pretence of yours, Daisy, are we permitted to find ourselves some food?' the earl asked.

'Yes, but I must stay at your side, if you please. I cannot risk Sir Reptile cutting me off,' Daisy replied. Mariah smiled sympathetically. It did not entirely suit her plans that so many people were around them all the time, but she could not abandon Daisy to Sir Lucas.

'Why may you not go in to supper with John Brent?' the earl asked.

'Why would I go into supper with him?' Daisy countered.

'Daisy.' The countess's voice cut across their bickering. 'I need you here.'

'Oh no,' Daisy moaned. 'I should have remembered that Anna is translating for the Spanish Ambassador and Mama is therefore unattended.' She left them and, with a bright smile in place, joined her mother's party.

'You look a little wistful, Miss Fox,' the earl said. 'Would you prefer to keep company with your papa?'

'No, sir. I sometimes can't help wondering what it would have been like had my mama survived. It passes.' She smiled. The earl's sensibility was a further surprise. Given the way he had trampled through his purposes before, he was displaying careful attention to the needs of herself and her papa while they were his guests.

'An understandable reaction,' he said. 'Although Mama and Daisy spar all the time, I think they enjoy a deep love. Let us take a turn in the garden before we find our meal. It is well-lighted, and there should be a sufficient number of my relatives circulating out there to avoid any threat of compromise to your reputation.'

They descended to the ground floor and passed along a wide hall towards the back of the house where two liveried footmen bowed the earl and his companion out onto the lawns. Honey-suckle scented the night darkness and it was quiet. Music from upstairs swelled into the air but there was no hubbub of voices. In fact, Mariah felt delightfully free from the press of people contained inside. The gardens must be very large, she thought, to allow this sense of space when there were others strolling about.

'You have an expressive face, Miss Fox,' the earl said, while they made their way along a gravel walk. 'Tell me what caused the revulsion when Sir Lucas explained his sister's absence.'

'I did not believe that she had fallen,' Mariah said quietly. 'I regret to say I wondered if Sir Lucas had injured her.'

'Why would you think that?'

'Why indeed?' Mariah asked, suddenly conscious of how great an insult she was levelling at someone she had met but three times, and only briefly on any occasion. 'I beg your pardon to have said something so inexcusable about your friend.'

'He is no friend of mine, and I saw him assault a child in the street very recently,' the earl said.

'Josh! That is why you were so very ready to help him.'

The earl nodded.

'John and I both witnessed the incident, but we were at too great a distance to intervene. He was saved from yet more serious injury by another passer-by.'

They took a few steps in silence. Mariah began to feel disorientated by events. Peter Sharp, for all his bullying ways, would never lift his hand to strike a woman. Or would he? She mulled over this new view of men so abruptly presented to her. Would she have been placing herself in danger by becoming Peter's wife?

Her papa had said he did not wish to entrust her to someone who would be threatened by her intellectual abilities and would steal her ideas. She herself had increasingly felt that Peter Sharp would stultify them. But if he could not suppress her intellectually, would he use his male strength to overcome her?

'Enough of Sir Lucas,' the earl said, cutting into her thoughts. 'Josh does well and Stephens may be able to find a place for him. I was explaining to you earlier how much I look forward to teaching you, Miss Fox. First there is the vow to love,' he said, taking her hand from his arm and bringing her fingers to his lips. They were warm and firm and Mariah took a moment to remove her hand from his.

'Your lordship should not be talking to me in this manner,' she protested. She was more concerned because her heart was beating so hard she could feel the pulses in her throat. It was only a half-hour since she had wanted to make the earl talk to her like this, but she had not factored the effect his words would have on her sensibilities.

'No? I had thought from the delightful acquiescence with my requests that your opposition to our union had been overcome,' he said, and Mariah was thankful that the darkness between the huge torches set about the gardens hid her expressive face for the moment. 'I was puzzled to begin with this evening, I must confess, but it did not take me long to work out your intentions, Mariah.' He led her off the gravel onto thick turf that sprang below her feet. When she would have pulled back, he tucked her arm tightly within the crook of his and simply kept walking.

Mariah had an unenviable choice. She could follow where his lordship led into the darkness below a stand of trees or she could make a fuss and draw unwanted eyes their way.

'Sir, this is unwise. How can you think that our progress is unobserved?' Mariah asked desperately as she tripped over a tree root. 'Lord Mellon!'

'My name is Tobias, Mariah. Please say it.'

'Please, Tobias,' she whispered. 'Please let us go back onto the paths where we can be seen respectably.'

'We will be seen, Mariah, when I wish us to be seen. I was talking about your intentions. Did you think to make me fall in love with you?' he asked. 'Have you made some plan and put it into action too quickly without testing its prospects of success?' When she did not reply, he spoke again. 'It is clear to me that Mr Fox has kept you too close, my dear. He has not allowed you that intercourse with other young women that would have educated you about the affairs of men and women.'

'How can you say so, sir? My papa has allowed me out into the world where I have enjoyed far more freedom than your own sister,' she protested.

'Yes, he has. Freedom can act as a shackle too, Mariah. You think that the only way to live your life is the one your parents follow. By letting you go, he draws you back.'

'Is this not what you are pursuing when you say you want a woman to replicate your mama's behaviour,' she said vehemently.

'Oh, Mariah, let us not quarrel. We will be married within the month. At least your papa's house contains plenty of books. You may practise throwing them.'

The instruments of the band fell silent and Mariah listened for the swell of voices that should take their place but there was none. A cold frisson of fear touched her heart. The earl had engineered her presence in the garden without any kind of escort and with none of his relatives to give them countenance.

'You have tricked me, sir,' she said.

'My beautiful girl, of course I have,' he said, as he pulled her into his embrace and kissed her.

9

Mariah heard her aunt's strident tones before she saw her. She groaned and turned over in her bed to bury her face in the pillows. Was it only three days since her world had been destroyed? Was it as long as three days since she had faced the entire company from the Blue Salon entering the gardens of Mellon House behind John Brent?

She threw her legs out straight as the frustrations of being hoodwinked by Tobias Longreach catapulted her whole body into spasm. How could she have been so naive? In such a clever move it took her breath away still, he had destroyed her reputation with all the people who mattered in the world of education. If she did not marry him now, she would never find work, nor would she find a husband.

'If you do not agree to go down, your

aunt says she's coming up, miss, even if Mr Wilson has to carry her,' Tilly said from her position inside the bedroom door.

Mariah screamed.

Tilly closed the door. 'Even with the pillows muffling, miss, that's going to carry down the stairwell,' she said briskly. 'I've laid out your brown stripe because I didn't think you'd want to inflame Mrs Wilson further by going down in one of the new gowns.'

Mariah rolled onto her side and glared at her maid. 'Then I do not agree with you for once,' she said. 'I am the one who has been wronged here and my aunt will not intimidate me. I have suffered at the hands of a master manipulator. She holds no fear.'

Tilly took a deep breath and folded the brown stripe over her arm. She pulled open the large oak cupboard and hung the dress away before lifting out a morning gown of palest cream silk. She pattered about the room, finding clean linen and fresh stockings, while Mariah splashed her face with warm water from her basin and tried to muster her thoughts.

Tilly dropped the dress over Mariah's head and knotted its ties behind. 'You can stand up now, miss. That dress is so beautiful with its piping around the sleeves an' all. I think there's a handkerchief of your mama's in just that shade of peacock blue,' she said, and rummaged in one of Mariah's drawers. Triumphantly, she waved the square of cloth around. 'Let me just pin this at your breast,' she said, and did so with a small brooch from the dresser.

Mariah gazed into the mirror and teased one or two curls around her chin. She smoothed the ribbons Tilly had inserted in her hair and straightened her posture. The girls had spent about twenty minutes making Mariah look as beautiful as they could, but it was simply making the best of things. She had been crying for three days. She'd sobbed in frustration, in anger, and in despair, but most of all because she knew she loved the earl. Without a shadow of a wisp of a doubt, she had fallen in love with him and he would never love her.

In the privacy of her room she had relived his kiss countless times. The power of his arms holding her against him thrilled her senses and drove thought from her mind. Where was the independently-brought-up miss who should have kicked his shins or bitten his mouth as his lips plundered hers? She was nowhere, and in her place Mariah had discovered another miss. She had found a girl like any other who revelled in the love of a strong gentleman.

And when she'd realised she was as vulnerable as any hopeful in Almack's rooms, she also had to realise she was ill-equipped to be the wife of an earl. Why had he done this to her? Why did he need to let his mother have her own way?

'I'll go down, Tilly,' she said.

⋆　⋆　⋆

'Well, Miss Mariah, what have you got to say about this farrago of nonsense I'm confronted with every time I call on anyone?' her aunt asked before Mariah was fully through the door of the morning room.

Mariah took a deep breath and inhaled a lungful of lilies and roses. She looked beyond her aunt's enormous figure and an astonishing sight met her gaze. Every receptacle they owned for the display of flowers was filled to bursting point. She clapped a hand over her mouth and turned slowly on the spot.

'That's an uncommonly expensive dress you're wearing,' her aunt said, as if the garment's very existence was a personal affront. 'I had hoped that the silly women had got it *all* wrong, but I see they may have some grounds for their suspicions.'

Mariah dragged her attention back to the people in the room. Her papa

184

was sitting on the very edge of his usual chair, as he always did when his sister called, and Mariah's heart was pierced by a shaft of compassion. It looked as if he hadn't slept while she had been keeping to her bed. Crossing the room and bending over him, she kissed his forehead. The doorbell clanged, but no one paid it the least attention.

'Are you feeling better, my love?' Jerome asked and stroked her arm.

'Much better, Papa, thank you. I am sorry to have been so indisposed.'

'Indisposed!' her aunt said. 'Why have you not been attending to your responsibilities, Mariah? Miss Ellyton tells me the urchins' class has been taught by Peter Sharp, and your girls at the Browning chapel by one of Mavis Shawditch's daughters. Is this what we brought you up for?'

'Good morning, Aunt Augusta,' Mariah said and dropped a curtsy. Her aunt had never encouraged intimacy, so she felt no need to embrace her.

'Uncle Arthur, it is good of you to bring my aunt to visit.'

Her aunt's news that Peter Sharp had seized the chance to take over her urchins' class distressed her, but there was so little prospect of her returning to it. Perhaps, she thought, it was better he made the attempt than that it faded away.

'Mariah, answer me.' Her aunt's voice, always loud, had become strident. 'I would not have raised such a vulgar subject, but Mr Sharp tells me he fears you have been led astray by the Earl of Mellon. If this is so, then we need to act immediately to remove you from further harm.' She wheezed out the words as her temper and her immense size began to overcome her breathing. 'My friend Miss Venables will undoubtedly welcome your skills at her ladies' seminary in Bath.'

'Mariah will not be going to work in Bath,' her papa said, while Augusta struggled to bring her breathing under control. Mariah watched her with detached interest, unable to look away, even when she heard the outer door open and confident footsteps cross the hall floor.

'Augusta feels the girl has over-stepped what is proper, Jerome,' Mariah's uncle offered as his wife was unable to speak. 'She thinks we need to act quickly to nullify the damage done to her reputation. Don't ye agree?'

'No, sir, I do not. Mariah, Lord Mellon has called every day since our return on Sunday evening and has sent a flower or two.' The ludicrous under-statement brought a smile to his face. 'He has spoken to me, my dear, as I'm sure you would expect . . . '

'Jerome,' Augusta spluttered, having found some breath. 'You cannot be contemplating a marriage with that man. Remember how he came into the title.'

Mariah looked at her father. 'He lost an elder brother to an infection following a sword wound,' she said. 'Was there anything suspicious about it, Papa?'

'It would seem that Leo Longreach was fighting with his brother when he was injured,' Jerome said.

'In other words, very suspicious,' Arthur Wilson said. 'The heir is killed off by the next in line.'

Mariah reached out to catch the side of a screen. Instantly, her hand was covered by a larger one. Tobias, she knew without looking. Comforting warmth drove out the cold of shock and she gasped. How she had ached for his touch while she lay prostrate. Now the moment was spoiled by a room pulsing with anger and the frustrated hopes of others.

'Good morning, Mariah,' he said. 'I am glad to see that your indisposition has been relieved.'

She bridled at the words whispered into her ear because he was telling her that he knew exactly what had caused her indisposition. How could he ignore the allegations being made about him in order to chastise her?

'It may return at any moment, sir, when I am overcome by the scent of so many blooms,' she said. His low chuckle inflamed her temper, but he was moving away from her and she took a seat as far away from the main group as possible.

The earl bowed to Jerome. 'Sir, I would be glad to meet your relatives.'

Mariah tried to understand the import of her uncle's words. Could there be any justification at all for such an accusation? She went over it in her head as introductions and formal exchanges were made. Was this why Constanzia wanted to retreat to Spain? Could she not bear the sight of her younger son because he had jealously killed off the heir standing in the way of his advancement?

'Mariah.' Jerome's voice cut through her troubled thoughts. 'Lord Mellon would like a few moments of your time.'

'Yes, Papa, of course. Shall we walk

out into the garden . . . ?' she began to say, when the memory of another garden rose in her mind's eye and stifled the words.

'Perhaps we should,' the earl said with firmness. He strode across to the double doors leading out to the house's small garden area, and after a quick appraisal threw them open. 'Mariah,' he said, and she rose.

They stepped through and the greenery surrounded them. She heard the doors clip shut, cutting off her aunt's stridency and replacing it with the drone of bees and the distant barking of a chained dog.

Tobias walked ahead of her down the short brick path that led to a gate from Jerome's property into the shared land in the square. He waited while she walked through and closed the gate behind them.

'You have no hat,' he said.

'The trees are in full leaf and will protect me from too much glare,' she answered.

He caught her hand and pulled it through his arm, making her walk at his side. She felt the heat of his body, heard the rhythmic noise of his boots, and inhaled his scent of clean linen and soap. Whatever this man had done, her heart was lost to him.

Tobias tensed, and she felt his muscles ripple as he struggled to relax. 'You acted with great presence of mind when my supposed crimes were alluded to by Mr Wilson. I am very glad you did not faint at my feet.'

'I thought it time to break the habit of having women fall at your feet. I am convinced it cannot be good for your character,' she said.

'Well said, Mariah. I have spoken with your father and he has graciously given me permission to address you.' He turned their footsteps into an arbour and set Mariah onto a bench there. 'I would be the happiest man alive, Mariah, if you will do me the honour of agreeing to be my wife.'

Mariah sat with her hands folded in

her skirts, and took a moment or two before lifting her eyes to his face. She saw how, even after all the machinations, he was nervous about her reply. She thought his neck-cloth looked tight and his breathing was a little agitated.

'Why are you nervous about my reply, Lord Mellon? You have done everything within your power to ensure I can give only one answer or must go to slave for Miss Venables in Bath,' she said.

'You did threaten to use such a ploy to escape from Peter Sharp's clutches,' he replied, and she felt his brown gaze search her face. 'That in itself is enough to make me nervous. Besides, you have just heard me accused of fratricide.'

'I have met Miss Venables on several occasions. She would not help me advance my ideas. She told my papa with some pride that her switch is kept beside her desk and used in every lesson. She was astonished to hear that he had never whipped me for stumbling over my Latin translation.'

'You and your papa are not alone in thinking children respond to kindness and encouragement, Mariah, but you are still in a minority.'

'I know it. Miss Venables would tell me so while reminding me I was there as an obligation,' she said. 'As to my uncle's assertion, he is not always able to marshal an argument that holds together. I think . . . ' She hesitated. 'I think he has probably misunderstood some gossip heard in his club.'

'That is very generous of you, my dear girl, and very trusting. Alas, gossip can be true in some elements. Leo and I *were* fencing and I tore into his thigh with an unsheathed blade. That is the wound that went bad,' Tobias said bleakly.

'An unsheathed blade? Surely brothers, or any friendly opponents, would have tipped blades?' Mariah protested before she could think. His revelation was as unpalatable as her suspicions of Sir Lucas.

Tobias ran his long fingers through

his hair and stepped away from the bench. Mariah watched with growing concern as he paced a little, seeming to debate something with himself. Abruptly, he stilled and turned toward her. His eyes sought out her troubled blue gaze and held it while he spoke.

'My brother was an unstable young man. He chose to risk his life in ways that were unnecessary and sometimes unpleasant for others around him. The day I injured him was in the early weeks after our father's death. Leo's mind seemed more turbulent than usual, and the fencing master would have cancelled the bout, but Leo insisted. He removed the tip from my blade under cover of a jerkin he threw off after our match began. I was still, waiting to one side for him to be ready again, and did not see what he had done until it was too late.'

'Who knows the truth?' Mariah asked. She was aghast at the implications of Tobias's words.

'The fencing master and John Brent,' Tobias said. 'And you.'

'Your mama? Daisy?' she asked, unable to believe that he had not defended himself from the accusations that must have followed.

'My mama may have her suspicions, but Daisy was still in the schoolroom and was told only that Leo fell on an unguarded sword,' Tobias said.

'And this is why you are so anxious to enable your mama's visit to Spain,' she said as so much of Tobias's life fell into place for her. 'You believe you did kill her son.'

'I have thought much about it. I believe my brother had a death wish, if there is such a thing. He took no joy in the pleasures of a life that was both privileged and blessed. My father's death opened up a vast deal of opportunity to him, but with the privileges came responsibilities such as he had never had to encompass.'

'You think coming into his inherit-ance caused him to seek out his own death?' Mariah asked, and felt tears well in her eyes.

'Yes, and in such a way that I am left shouldering that responsibility for him as well as having to take his life's path,' Tobias said, his face a mask. Mariah could not tell if he was angry with the unstable young man or had come to accept his fate. 'So, Mariah, you will see that it is of great importance to me to marry a woman I feel will not only be a helpmeet but who will bring vigour into the family bloodline.'

Mariah stifled a laugh. 'You have considered me as if I were a brood mare, sir?'

'Oh, I have, Mariah,' he said, breathing the words quietly. He reached out, and she felt his hand touch the side of her cheek and move around to cup her jaw. 'But the stallion knows only animal instinct. I am captivated by so much more. Will you marry me?'

'Yes, my lord, I will,' she said. The words were out and she was caught.

She had been caught that day in the yards when he lifted her into his arms. It had needed the playing out of this week of drama to make her accept it.

10

'You have secured a plum prize, Miss Fox. I congratulate you,' the nasal voice said quietly at her side. 'Of course, there was little competition, as the earl is removed from the lists of suitable young men kept by Society ladies and their mamas.'

Mariah knew immediately that Sir Lucas Wellwood had seized the chance created by Tobias's absence to accost her. It was their first outing together since the announcement of their forthcoming nuptials had appeared in the public papers. The rooms at Lady Melchambers's mansion house were crowded and it had not been possible to identify any of their friends before Tobias departed in search of refreshment. She was unprotected.

'Good evening, Sir Lucas,' she said. 'Is your sister with you or has she suffered another fall?' Instantly, she regretted the words and their implications, but it was too late to recall them.

'Thank you for your concern. My sister is here, although not with me. She is the guest of Lady Barlow and her son, Reginald.' Wellwood studied his fingernails before raising his distinctive eyes to hers. 'Amarinta does have a tendency to fall. I am sorry for it.'

'Perhaps it is something she will grow out of.'

'Or perhaps it is something she may avoid by altering her behaviour,' said Wellwood, and he narrowed his eyes yet more. Mariah felt a chill cover her arms with goosebumps, although the rooms were hot and stuffy. 'I wonder how long it will take Mellon to bring *you* to heel, my beauty?'

Mariah stared in horror at the man as the meaning of his utterance became clear. 'Lord Mellon would never . . . '

'Exercise his rights to beat you into obedience? I think you may mistake the nature of the beast, my dear Miss Fox.

You are not marrying a man of the educated, emasculated classes such as your papa. You are marrying an aristocrat whose word is law and above the law. It is well known his brother did not die from natural causes.' Wellwood curled his lip disdainfully. 'Not that *I* hold such things against him. Some in the political world move too far towards removing the liberty of the individual.'

'So you did assault your sister,' she said, her voice reduced to a whisper.

'No, Miss Fox. I *chastised* my sister for stupidly offending Lady Daisy. I knew as soon as she repeated the chit's words about Mellon's intentions towards you that we had lost that prize. No matter how hard the girl worked to re-instate herself in his regard, she would have an enemy in the family working against the match.' He moved away from her slightly and Mariah caught sight of Tobias easing through the throng. 'Yes, I see him too. Remember this, you stupid bitch: he will have what he wants of you. He will have a wife, an heir, and a hostess. There is no place in your new existence for the teaching of brats who should have been exterminated at birth.'

Wellwood slid away into the press of guests and was gone from sight before Tobias reached her side. She felt the blood begin to pulse back into her shaken being. He *was* a reptile. Across the room she watched Amarinta smile up into the face of a large youth of flabby appearance. Mariah saw the girl's slow smile as this person slid his hand around her and let his fingers lie on the swell of her buttocks.

'Mariah,' Tobias said, holding a glass of lemonade out to her. 'You are studying Miss Wellwood and her friends.'

'Miss Wellwood does not seem to object to the gentleman's indelicate touch,' she said, and took a sip of the drink.

'My sister tells me that the Wellwoods are in dire need of funds.' Tobias was silent for a moment or two as he tried to secure a gap in the throng to see what Mariah had seen. 'The youth she is with is the only son of the late Sir Reginald Barlow. He is wealthy from the proceeds of his father's mills,' Tobias said quietly.

'This may have come about because you have decided to marry me, my lord,' Mariah said. 'As Sir Lucas is so preoccupied with the peerage, it suggests their needs are very dire. Miss Wellwood may be sacrificing herself.'

'Mariah, my love, has something happened to upset you?' Tobias asked.

'No,' she said quickly. She would not let Tobias know how Wellwood had spoken to her. She would not dwell on it because that would mean the man had achieved his aim of destroying her happiness in her forthcoming marriage. Tobias, Earl of Mellon was an honourable man. He would not act as Wellwood had done.

It was much later, as she drifted into

sleep, that she registered Tobias had called her *my love*.

* * *

Mariah watched her papa sleep in his study chair the following morning, and experienced another flash of concern about his health. He seemed to be asleep in the daytime far more often than would be expected of a man of his age, but when she asked him how he went on he was dismissive.

'Perhaps I over-tax my strength, my love, when I sit into the night reading and writing. But truth be told, I find it difficult to sleep then,' he had said only yesterday. 'I would not have you worry, however, and once you and the earl are married, I will consult a physician.'

She recalled the conversation now as she descended to the morning room to wait for Daisy, and was even less satisfied with it than she had been at the time. Her papa often succeeded in putting off unpleasant things by appearing to take an initiative. Why had he thought about consulting a physician? Had he already consulted one? There would have been ample opportunity for him to see someone while she was teaching her classes and out of the house for several hours at a time.

The doorbell clanged, interrupting her thoughts, and Josh, newly installed as their boot-boy, scurried to answer. Mrs Burtles had graciously sent Letty and Josh along from Grosvenor Square to increase the staff in Redde Place. Mariah had appointed Tilly to be her lady's maid and the girl was working hard. She was determined to learn as much about her new duties as her sisters could teach her in the short weeks before Mariah's wedding.

The whole of Mariah's existence was in turmoil, and she struggled to find any time in which to keep up her reading of the newspapers or the educational pamphlets she had once studied so avidly. It was a matter of interest to her, how little she missed them while she pored over fashion plates and visited warehouses with Daisy in preparation for buying her wedding clothes.

Who was this caller, she wondered. People on the fringes of the *ton* had been calling regularly since the announcement of her marriage, and she had to be selective in who she allowed to know she was 'at home'. It was all very strange and very disturbing, but there were many people as desperate as the Wellwoods. They wanted to claim acquaintance with the future Countess of Mellon.

Josh came into the room with a visiting card on his tray. He bowed a little stiffly.

'It be Miss Wellwood, miss,' he said.

'Really?' Mariah took the card from Josh's tray and contemplated the name engraved there. *Amarinta Wellwood*. What could the girl want with her?

'Ask Miss Wellwood to come through please, Josh.' She waited while Amarinta was shown in, and the two young women studied each other in silence for a moment or two. Mariah could not bring herself to ask Amarinta to sit down, and so they faced each other from opposite ends of the worn carpet square set between the chairs.

'It is very good of you to allow me to visit you, Miss Fox,' Amarinta said, speaking first. 'I would not have been surprised if you had preferred not to do so, but a person of your known intellectual curiosity must be intrigued.'

'So you have not come with any spirit of reconciliation in mind?' Mariah said.

'Have we quarrelled, Miss Fox? I was not aware of it. But I do not wish you well. Your arrival in Lord Mellon's life has spoiled my life for the time being.' She took a letter tied with a length of red ribbon from her reticule. 'However, it is not about that that I am here.'

'What possible harm have I done to you?' Mariah protested, shocked afresh by the way the girl's face took on an entirely different aspect when she was roused. 'I hope that Sir Lucas did not offer further violence after our conversation last night.'

Amarinta fixed her green gaze on Mariah's face. 'I cannot think what you mean, Miss Fox. I do trust you are not bruiting it abroad that my brother is anything other than a loving and concerned guardian who acts in my best interests.'

'He admitted it,' Mariah said baldly, refusing to be intimidated by the girl's veiled threat. 'He called it 'chastisement', and said you might avoid it by changing your behaviour.'

'Whatever my brother has said on this subject, I will deny. I am to be married by special licence in three days' time to Reginald Barlow of Newcastle-upon-Tyne. Lady Barlow, his mama, is not the most refined of women, but she is respectable. She would not be able to countenance any scandal attaching to Lucas, and for another two years of Reginald's minority, she holds his purse-strings,' Amarinta said. She tugged the hems of her gloves while she gathered her thoughts.

'This has little to do with me, Miss Wellwood, although I wish you every happiness in your marriage.'

'If I were in your position, I would be wishing me every happiness I *deserved* in my forthcoming marriage,' the girl said, looking around. Mariah realised she wished to sit down and reluctantly proposed that they should do so.

'Thank you, Miss Fox,' Amarinta said slowly. 'Before I marry Reginald, there is one last undertaking I must complete for Lucas. Daisy Mellon has long been his preferred choice of bride.' The girl's lids came down over the green eyes.

'Daisy? I have heard nothing from Lord Mellon to indicate that there is any foundation for such a supposition. Indeed, Daisy is to travel to Spain with Lady Mellon,' Mariah said. She remembered the way Sir Lucas had run his gaze over Daisy outside the modiste's salon and shuddered. Was there more to his behaviour than insolence? She started. Did Lucas Wellwood really believe he could secure Daisy's hand?

'Daisy Mellon is in possession of a large settlement which my brother would find very useful in his present financial embarrassment. She offered it to that idiot Brent, of course, in the hope it would make him ask for her hand, but he turned it down. Something about not living on his wife's money,' Amarinta said.

Mariah stifled a gasp. She had not heard this snippet of information, but it did not surprise her. John Brent and Daisy sparked off each other in a way that could lead one to think there was deep feeling between them.

'Surely it does not surprise you to learn Mr Brent would feel as you suggest?' she asked in order to cover her momentary lapse. Although she had been out of charity with John Brent since he organised Tobias's ruse in the gardens at Grosvenor Square, he had impressed her with his deep friendship for the earl.

'I think there are many men in the position of my brother and Mr Brent, who would not have much regard for a nicety such as where the money comes from.'

'There is no possibility of Daisy accepting your brother, Miss Wellwood.' Mariah knew her incredulity was plain to hear, but she could not help it.

'Of course not. That is why he will abduct her and seduce her,' Amarinta said. 'Afterwards, Daisy will have no choice but to accept him, and her fortune will pass into his hands.'

'How can your brother make such plans when he has no funds to secure helpers? You must know how well protected Lady Daisy is,' Mariah said desperately. Was there no end to the nightmare this brother and sister trailed with them? 'Why are you telling this story to me? Why not go to Lord Mellon?'

'Lord Mellon would not agree to see me alone. Daisy has been my friend, and I would not like her to be forced to marry Lucas. While, as I have said, I would deny anything he was accused of in public, I know he has an unpredictable temper and an autocratic disposition. His wife's life would be miserable and possibly short.'

Mariah clasped her hand across her mouth in shock. She felt the room swim and within seconds Amarinta had risen and was holding water at her lips. She drank a few sips and, taking the glass in shaking fingers, sat back against the arm of her chair.

'I recommend that you do not take this information to Lord Mellon or John Brent either,' Amarinta said and fixed her gaze on Mariah. 'If you have any regard for Daisy's safety, you must listen to the proposal I've brought from my brother. Without *your* cooperation, however unwillingly offered, she is in grave danger.' Amarinta smoothed down the front of her gown as if she had offered an opinion on the flowers Mariah might choose to dress her front room. She returned to her chair, and again fixed her green gaze on Mariah's pale face.

'There are ways of making sure a young lady is on her own or separated from friends, particularly when that young lady is full of life and spirits like Daisy. It is not difficult in our dark streets. As to my brother's lack of funds . . . ' She shrugged. 'You must understand that many will join him on the promise of riches to come, or just because they want to lay hands on an upper-class lady. They would enjoy treating her roughly or worse.'

Mariah rose as the girl's words drew an unpalatable picture for her. She had only ventured a short way off the respectable streets seeking children for her classes, and knew that once around a corner or two there would be alleys and courtyards where all sorts of desperate people held sway. She had glimpsed them but never penetrated into their depths.

'You have evidently come here to

explain how I might prevent this outrage against Lady Daisy,' she said.

'My brother is right, Miss Fox. You have an uncommonly sharp understanding,' Amarinta said. She lifted the letter she had placed on a side table while she helped Mariah to some water. 'You will steal the Mellon tiara when it is brought to you on the morning of your wedding.'

'I cannot do such a thing,' Mariah protested, but Amarinta ignored her outburst and continued.

'The instructions on how to proceed are written here. I had a clerk copy them out because my hand would be recognised by anyone from the Mellon household,' Amarinta said. 'But in any case, you will burn the missive before I leave.'

'Even if I were alone with the tiara, which I do not think I will be, how can I turn up at the church without its absence being noticed immediately?'

'Try to remember that Daisy Mellon's fate lies in your hands, Miss Fox.'

213

Mariah subsided onto her chair once more. She was beginning to understand what it meant to be powerless, and she did not like the feeling.

'My brother has worked out all the details. He had expected it to be me marrying the earl, and had laid his plans accordingly. He well knew the earl would not make him an allowance, and while he thought my own allowance as the countess would ease his immediate embarrassments, he knew he needed something a lot more daring,' Amarinta said. Mariah was again struck by the girl's calmness while she explained her brother's deceit and dishonesty. 'The Mellon tiara, once broken down into its individual stones, will enable him to live very comfortably for many years.'

'You are so calm in the face of these monstrous crimes,' Mariah said.

'I have learned that my brother will not be denied. With my hoped-for marriage to the earl in view, he had a copy of the tiara made some time ago while he was flush from the gaming tables. It is a very good copy. You will substitute it for the real thing. Remember that Daisy Mellon's fate is in your hands.'

'You do not regard kidnapping and seduction as sufficiently scandalous to upset your future mama-in-law?' Mariah asked in disbelief. She heard the servants moving around in the front part of the house but knew they would not disturb their mistress while she had a guest.

'I certainly do. That is why I have pushed Reginald into seeking a special licence in order that we may be married before you are,' Amarinta said. 'Living in the North, I need not pay as much attention to Lucas as has been necessary while I am dependent on him. Once I am carrying her grandchild, Lady Barlow will find herself able to discount anything she reads in the newspapers about my brother.'

'Reginald Barlow is to be your escape route,' Mariah murmured. Where, she thought desperately, would she find her own? One thing was absolutely clear to her. She could not marry the earl if there was such a crime against him clouding her past. 'I cannot do this.'

'Perhaps you think so now, Miss Fox, but time will show you the error of trying to thwart my brother.' Amarinta undid the ribbon. 'This is his idea of humour,' she said, and dropped it to the floor. 'Daisy and I used to exchange our girlish confidences tied up with red ribbon.' She spread the sheet.

'Now, I will read these instructions to you because I see you are toying with ideas of frustrating Lucas's plans and I will only rest easily if I have seen this damned thing burn. Listen carefully, Miss Fox.' She began to read.

'*When the Mellon tiara is brought by representatives of the earl's lawyers, accept it in your room.*

'*The lawyers will send two men wearing the Mellon livery and a*

216

woman dressed as a wedding guest, with the item. The men will check your room for hidden thieves and then wait outside but the woman will enter and stay with you. Her job is to fit the tiara into your hair and attach the veil. She is the person you must concern yourself with.

'You will have a jug of cordial made up and will have contaminated it with a herbal preparation which will be delivered to you the day before the wedding, in a parcel of books from Hatchards' of Piccadilly. Press some of the cordial on the female escort. Within minutes the cordial will make it necessary for the female to ask permission to withdraw into your closet as a matter of urgency. Do not worry that the woman may die. My plan cannot work if she should do so.

'While the wretched woman relieves her stomach pains, exchange the false tiara and the genuine one. You do not need to know how the copy will come into your possession, lest you be tempted to inform his lordship or anyone else, but you will have it in time.

'After the wedding party, with its three escorts, departs for the Church, the real tiara will be collected.

'Read this letter and remember what is set out here. Now burn it.'

Amarinta set it alight over the empty hearth and waited while it burned.

11

'The Earl of Mellon, Miss Mariah,' Josh announced.

'Good morning, Mariah,' Tobias said as he entered the morning room where Mariah had remained after Amarinta's departure. 'Daisy has an indisposition and begs your forgiveness. She sent me in her stead to offer any assistance you might need.'

Mariah was grateful that Daisy was ill, because it allowed her to have a serious expression without Tobias asking for an explanation. She could mask her unhappiness, bewilderment, and fear behind concern over her friend's illness.

'I am very sorry to hear that, my lord. Does she keep to her room?' Mariah asked. She allowed her gaze to rest on Tobias's face, and drank in the planes and shadows that made him such a handsome man. How could she contemplate life without him? What could she do to defeat the odious, evil baronet?

'Miss Mariah, Miss Mariah.' Tilly threw herself into the room with such impatience she knocked Josh over. 'It's the master!'

Mariah was on her feet and heading up the stairs before Tilly had finished speaking. Her heart thundered blood in her ears. She reached the landing and caught sight of her papa sunk lifeless in his chair.

'No, please God, no,' Mariah breathed the words. Jerome was still, and she noticed he'd been a little sick. She joined Cook beside his chair and reached a shaking hand to touch his skin.

'Does he breathe?' Tobias asked as he strode across the room. 'Do you have a mirror?'

Tilly sped off, to return within seconds brandishing a small hand-mirror from Mariah's dressing table. The earl held it below Jerome's nose and was able to show Mariah a covering of condensation. Power melted from her legs as she understood what she saw. Her papa was not dead but unconscious. He lived.

'It may be nothing more than a fever,' the earl said encouragingly, but Mariah heard the undertone of concern and saw again the way Tobias looked at her papa. He did not believe it was a passing fever. 'Let Josh and I lift him into his bed. Then I will send to our doctors for assistance. Is your shoulder up to this, lad?'

Mariah stepped back while they grappled with Jerome's long body and half-carried, half-dragged him across the landing into his room. Tilly and Cook helped Josh undress their master and settle him into his bed.

She sat at his side until a physician arrived, and only gave way to that gentleman's quiet insistence. She would have waited outside Jerome's room while the examination of the patient took place, but Tobias guided her downstairs into the big room and across it to the long windows open onto the gardens.

'Come, Mariah,' the earl said gently. 'Let us take some air while your papa is examined. It will restore you after the shock of the morning.'

Mariah allowed herself to be led into the garden and took a deep breath of fresh air.

'Papa has kept the upstairs tightly shut for several days,' she said as the earl offered her an arm and they began to walk around the back garden with a measured tread. 'I have developed a headache in the atmosphere while waiting for the doctor.'

'Has your papa expressed any concern over his health?' the earl asked.

'No. The concern has been all mine. I should have insisted he see a physician rather than allow him to fob me off with promises to make a consultation after we are married.'

'It is often thus, I think,' Tobias said quietly. 'I do not think you should berate yourself. I have seen a little of your papa in these recent weeks, and I imagine he does not pursue any activity that gets between him and his work. Even his own health,' he added.

Mariah saw the fond smile hover around Tobias's mouth, and it eased the pain of her guilt. He was exactly right. Jerome dithered until a problem resolved itself. There was nothing she could have done to make him see a doctor more quickly.

She stilled their progress and, reaching up onto her toes, kissed her betrothed shyly. She felt the rasp of his beard as she sank back, and sensed the shock her actions had caused him. At her side his muscles, usually so supple and strong, were still and taut.

'You have set my mind at rest a little, and I am grateful,' she said. He said nothing and Mariah began to wonder if her behaviour was inexcusable even between those who would soon know each other as intimately as was possible.

'Mariah,' he said at last, 'you do me a

great honour to entrust me with your kiss. I am not unaware that I insulted you in Grosvenor Square.'

Mariah remembered the kisses they'd shared then in the dark shelter of the gardens and the way hot chills had run through her untutored body as he'd gathered her against him and plundered her mouth. Was it an insult? In the closely-guarded society they both inhabited she knew he was right. In the depths of her soul, she longed for the privacy of their marriage.

He was watching her very carefully, and she felt heat creep up her neck and flush her cheeks. She was uncertain of how she should answer him or how she should behave. The absence of her mama had never been more clearly borne in on her. Memory of her mama inevitably brought her back to her poor father perhaps fighting for breath upstairs.

'You do not believe it is a passing fever, do you?' she asked.

Tobias urged her on again. 'I am

afraid I don't, my love,' he said. 'I have myself seen the flash of pain cross his features when he has been unable to prevent it. I am sorry to say, I think your papa may be very ill indeed.'

'Thank you for being honest with me,' she said. 'It is the conclusion I had come to.' Mariah knew then that she had realised for some time how ill her papa was, but had played along with his insistence that it was his age. That was why she had been shocked but not surprised to see him earlier. She was expecting his death.

Josh called to them from the house and they went in.

⋆　⋆　⋆

As Tobias prepared to leave Redde Place, he was far more troubled than when he had arrived with the intention of accompanying Mariah to a shoe warehouse. What had started as a normal morning for a man betrothed to be married had rapidly turned into anything but.

225

He was glad to know that the medical man did not believe Mr Fox was in imminent danger. Indeed, he had offered advice on changes Mr Fox might make in his daily living that would be beneficial. At the same time, Mr Fox had become agitated when it was mooted that they postpone the wedding, and so it was still scheduled to take place in under three weeks' time.

Tobias was worried. Mariah had been almost grateful to mention the postponement of their wedding, despite her shy kiss in the garden and the flash of searing memory he'd seen in her brilliant eyes when he referred to his kisses on the earlier occasion. His bride was unafraid of married intimacy or of him, he was sure; but she was afraid of something, and she had not imparted to him what it was.

'Your lordship,' Josh said, as he held out his hat and gloves. The boy's voice brought Tobias back into the present with a start. When did the servants ever address him? It must be very important.

'Josh?' he enquired, and bent his head to one side to let the boy know he would listen.

'Begging your lordship's pardon, but that young lady that came here this morning,' the boy said, and clammed up as if those few words had used all his daring for the present.

Tobias suppressed a shudder. What now?

'Did Miss Fox have a visitor?' he asked, hating the need to know that prodded him with the heat of a needle readied to lance a boil.

'She did, my lord. It were that Miss Wellwood what's sister to the baronet. She came in a closed carriage and she upset Miss Fox, she did.' The boy shuffled his feet. 'I don't think that's right, your lordship. She's a good mistress, Miss Fox.'

Tobias felt his sinews contract with sudden, urgent fear. What possible business did Amarinta Wellwood have here? Was it her own, or — more likely — was she on some devilish ploy set up by her brother? He remembered the sober nature of Mariah's welcome. She'd been quiet even before he told her of Daisy's indisposition.

'I didn't listen at the door, your lordship,' Josh was saying, and Tobias took heart.

'Of course not, Josh,' he said encouragingly. The lad had a 'but' up his sleeve, or Tobias was the slow-top Lucas clearly took him for.

'But I did have business in the front part of the mornin' room, and I couldn't help to hear the lady's words 'cos she was readin' from a letter. She said it was a letter, and there's a ribbon in there now like Miss Daisy's letters sometimes have at the big 'ouse. It was slow and clear. Like it is when Miss Fox reads in class.'

Tobias recalled the faint smell of burning that wafted from the room as the door opened to admit him earlier. Before he'd had the chance to ask

Mariah about it, Jerome's illness had intruded.

The household remained upstairs or in the kitchen, busy with their own ways of ministering to Mr Fox. The young servant and his master were alone in the hall. Tobias's stomach muscles clenched. How could he do the thing he was contemplating? Where would his credentials as a gentleman be if he invited Josh to repeat what he had overheard?

As if he sensed his master's dilemma, Josh rushed into speech and, with tiny hesitations and a little stumbling over longer words, he recounted an approximation of the whole.

No wonder Lucas instructed his sister to ensure it was burned, Tobias thought when the boy had finished.

He nodded to Josh, accepted his hat and gloves, and departed.

★ ★ ★

Mariah heard the front door close below her and stepped onto the landing where the window would allow her to catch a glimpse of Tobias striding down Redde Place before he turned left or right at the end. She saw him take a few steps, then falter, before heading determinedly on toward Grosvenor Square.

She puzzled a little over his hesitation, but when Tilly called to her from her papa's room, she set aside the niggle of doubt planted in her brain. Her papa was her main concern for the present.

'Mariah,' Jerome said from the depths of his bed. Cook and Tilly had piled him with blankets and wrapped his thin frame in shawls. He looked far less imposing than he had in the black suiting he favoured for his day-wear. 'Mariah.'

'I'm here, Papa,' she said, forcing a cheerfulness she could not feel into her voice. 'Are you comfortable?'

'Do I look comfortable?' he asked with unusual asperity. 'It is very nearly midsummer, child. Are you and these women trying to cook me?'

'Of course not,' she said, and gave a genuine laugh at the seriousness of his enquiry. 'You were chilled as you came round and it seemed natural to wrap you up. Let me help,' she offered as her father began to struggle with the layers of cloth smothering him.

'That's better. Off you go, Tilly, I want a few words with Miss Mariah,' Jerome said. 'Now, Mariah, sit here please.' He patted the bed beside him, and she sank into it, taking his hand in her own.

She studied the papery, thin skin, and the large veins criss-crossing it. When had her father passed from middle age into old age? Why hadn't she noticed the changes that were now so obvious?

'You will be chastising yourself for letting me get into this state, my dear, and truly there's nothing you could have done differently. I am an old man. I was a lot older than your mama, and it was the greatest misfortune that she was taken so early,' Jerome said peaceably.

'I accept that I couldn't have done anything to make you consult a physician, Papa, but why will you not allow us to postpone the wedding? It will be an unnecessary tax on your strength.'

'Nonsense. I will be no more and no less involved in buying wedding clothes than I would have been. All I am required to do is find the strength to walk you up the aisle,' Jerome said with maddening logic. 'I will manage that with great pride.'

The words were too much for Mariah, and she burst into a fit of tears that had her papa struggling to take her in his arms. She felt his hand pat her shoulder and the warmth of his embrace helped to calm her.

'I beg your pardon, Papa,' she said at last.

'Mariah, is there any reason you should not accept the Earl of Mellon's suit? I am anxious to have you settled in good domestic circumstances before I die, but I would not force you to marry if there was any reason against it.' Jerome fixed his intelligent gaze on her face, and she schooled her expression to give nothing away of the real reasons she was so unhappy.

'I am more than content to marry Tobias, Papa. It is your health that troubles me,' she said.

'Then we are agreed. The wedding will take place as arranged. Now, please call off the women and allow Josh to attend to me. I need something to read.'

'Papa, the doctor said . . . '

'I heard what the fellow said, and I know that if I am forced to lie here in indolence, I will rapidly reach the state of apoplexy his lordship tells me he worries over for his mama.'

'Tobias told you that?' she said wonderingly. 'He does feel at home here.'

★   ★   ★

Mariah descended to the morning room and caught sight of Lucas Wellwood's infernal red ribbon. Tobias probably didn't see it, she thought, because Tilly came so soon after his arrival with the news about Papa. In a few weeks' time, Tobias might well ask her who wrote to her and what the missives contained. It was the kind of thing they would want to learn about each other, but any husband would be intrigued to know who sent letters wrapped in red ribbon. Hadn't Amarinta said that anyone from Grosvenor Square would recognise her handwriting? It was clearly a household where secrets were discouraged.

The words of Wellwood's letter had been well-chosen, so no one could misunderstand the instructions set out. There were few and they were prescriptive. She had no difficulty remembering them.

When the Mellon tiara is brought by representatives of the earl's lawyers, accept it in your room . . .

Mariah dropped the ribbon onto her side table and rang the bell. When Josh came into the room she asked him to call a hackney cab for her from the stand at the end of Redde Place. The boy's eyes strayed to the ribbon and Mariah had to still the instinct to grab it up and crush it into her pocket.

'Where shall I say you will be going, miss?' Josh asked.

'Why, to Mellon House, Josh. I must enquire after Lady Daisy's health. Now that Mr Fox has seen a medical man, I feel I may leave him for an hour,' she said. She tossed the ribbon into the grate then, but there was no fire burning, so it lay in a whirl of colour against the ashes and twists of paper and kindling the boy had set earlier.

'Ask Tilly to be ready to accompany me,' she said.

Fifteen minutes later, the two young women, suitably dressed for a morning call, set off in a hired hackney. Mariah could feel the suspicion Josh directed at them, and so waited until the carriage was out of sight of the house before she rapped on the roof with her parasol.

'Are we not going to Mellon House, then, Miss Mariah?' Tilly asked.

'No,' Mariah said sharply, and gave the driver further directions.

She sat back against the cushions, which were not as clean as those of the Mellon town carriage, and studied the lines of disapproval marring Tilly's face.

'If I ever discover that you have told anyone about this expedition, you will be looking for employment elsewhere,' she said, and tried to ignore the expression of hurt disbelief. Then she added, 'It's better this way, Tilly.'

* * *

In Mellon House, Tobias noticed the way John Brent pulled at the hem of his waistcoat as he came into his study behind Stephens. He wondered for a fleeting moment if Brent was nervous.

'John,' he said evenly. 'I am glad you are come to me because I was going to seek you out as a matter of some urgency.' Tobias was astonished when his words raised a bright red flush across John Brent's face and neck. There was something troubling John. Had he discovered some of the events he was about to discuss with him? 'Are you quite well, man? You've taken on so much colour. Have you been eating strawberries?' Tobias asked. He knew the Brent family all suffered if they consumed them.

'No, I have not. I wonder that you have learned of my purpose in calling on you in this formal way. I had not thought that the news was out yet.' Tobias heard the tetchiness in his friend's tone.

'It is unusual for you to call on me formally. Have your circumstances changed then?'

'This is going all wrong before we are even finished saying good morning,' John complained. He paced the rug and stopped abruptly to glare at Tobias. 'I had not thought that you would make it difficult for me.'

'Have you come to ask my permission to address Daisy?' Tobias spoke the thought even as it firmed up in his mind. Relief that one of his troubled responsibilities was about to be resolved eased the pain of his discovery in Redde Place.

'Yes, I have.'

'I do not wish to make anything difficult for you, John. Daisy has long ago agreed that she would marry the man she loved on the settlement Papa left her. Together with her small inheritance from our grandmamma, you will be very comfortable.' He stood up and came around the desk to shake hands with John. 'I would not trust my sister to any fortune hunter, but I know that you are not such, and I wish you every happiness. Truth be told, I wondered why the two of you are so often together but quarrelling; apart, but asking after the other. I have been slow. No doubt my mama and your sisters have been waiting for the announcement.'

John turned away from Tobias's outstretched hand and walked to the window where he gazed out onto the garden. Tobias drew himself up in amazement.

'Men have been called out for lesser insults than the refusal of their hand,' Tobias said quietly. 'I must conclude that I have trodden on your sensibilities.'

'This fashion for ladies, particularly young ladies, to set themselves up as arbiters of acceptable behaviour, is not entirely to my taste,' John said, without turning back into the room. 'I told Daisy that I thought her too forward, and that I would not seek her hand until my circumstances came about. That was when she began to talk about the Spanish nobleman.'

'Ah, yes,' Tobias agreed, 'and about travelling to Spain with Mama. At least your decision will spare her that. I cannot think Daisy would enjoy the rigours of the sea passage and the miles of unmade road on the Peninsula, as much as she has convinced herself she would.'

'Tobias,' John said, and at last turned back from his contemplation of a large geranium, 'may we start this interview over, if you please?'

Tobias nodded, and indicated a chair close to the table where he kept a decanter and glasses. He poured them both some brandy.

'Now, man — your story.'

'I have recently stumbled on some chests and safe boxes m'father had stored in the attics at Brent House. Papers I found in those boxes suggested that he had made a purchase of land in the Northeast after I was born, with the intention of passing it on to a second son. As you know, Mama presented him with three daughters but no other son,' John said, and sipped a little brandy.

'The Northeast. An attractive area?' Tobias asked.

'According to my man of business, it is passing pleasant on the surface, but it is what lies beneath the land that has changed my circumstances, Toby.' John set the glass unfinished onto the table. Tobias could feel his excitement as if it were indeed palpable. 'There is coal. I have already begun taking action by engaging a mine manager and engineers. I will be able to support a wife before m'godfather dies, and I will be able to settle something on m'sisters.'

'Congratulations, John. I am pleased for you, and I will do everything in my power to make Daisy give up her trip to Spain.' Tobias smiled broadly. 'I know how pride must have made it impossible for you to ask for Daisy's hand before. I apologise if I have been insensitive.'

John stood up and the men shook hands. Tobias set himself apart and drew breath. Perhaps this wasn't the time to inflict his discovery of Mariah's treachery on his friend.

'Now, my lord,' John said. 'What urgent business did you have to tell me?'

'Why, it was very little, really. I would not trouble you when you wish to speak with Daisy,' he said. 'Although, I am sorry to have to tell you that she keeps to her room today, with an indisposition possibly caused by some oysters she ate at a theatre party last night.'

'How does she do?' John asked with the new licence his position gave him.

'She sent down for toasted crumpets an hour since, so I think we can conclude she is on the mend,' Tobias said. He slumped into his chair. How could he contemplate life without Mariah? How could he give up the right to ask after her health?

'Damn it,' he said, and felt John's startled gaze rake his face. 'I must tell someone what I have discovered, else I shall go mad.'

*   *   *

Mariah sat in Mr Routledge's outer office. Tilly gazed around them in frank curiosity, but Mariah was agitated to the point where she had to press herself down into the over-stuffed armchair she had been offered. Even that was only available after an armload of papers and tattered files were cleared away. Tilly balanced on a three-legged stool. Mr Routledge's surroundings did not inspire confidence.

Behind the door of his inner sanctum, the ladies could hear frantic activity. Mr Routledge had come out briefly to ascertain that the clerk had heard her name correctly and he had indeed received a visit from Miss Mariah Fox. Then he had hauled the clerk by the sleeve of his coat into the inner room and started moving things.

Mariah picked at the fringe of her reticule, loosening it and causing a fall of threads and fluff. She let the stuff lie on her gown and then picked at that, forming it into tiny balls.

'That Miss Wellwood has upset you no end, hasn't she?'

'It is nothing, Tilly. Nothing I won't be able to deal with if I can learn a few facts from Mr Routledge,' she said, and even to her own ears it sounded hopeless. When would she get to speak to the man? Why did Routledge think he needed to clean house simply to advise her? She stood up and crossed to the panelled door of his inner office. Raising her parasol she knocked. The door opened, and Routledge's clerk escaped into the outer office with a huge basket of overflowing paper and parchments tied with dusty black ribbon.

'Come in, Miss Fox,' Routledge said as he wiped the seat of a chair with his pocket handkerchief. 'We normally go out to the client, Miss Fox. You take us by surprise. Indeed, I cannot think when I ever had a lady visitor. Mrs Routledge will be most astonished when I tell her of the circumstances this evening.'

Mariah stepped into the room and turned to Tilly, who had risen when the door opened.

'Wait there, Tilly,' she said, and heard

Routledge close the door behind her.

'Now, Miss Fox, how can Routledge and Son help you?' the lawyer asked, and Mariah waited while he lowered himself carefully into the chair behind his huge desk. It was feet-deep in bundles of papers, and she tried to believe he knew what each of those bundles held. If his recall was as muddled as his surroundings, then her journey might prove fruitless.

'I am, as my father has told you, engaged to be married to the Earl of Mellon,' she began, and when Routledge would have started on a round of congratulations, she held up her hand for him to keep quiet. 'I find that marrying the earl is proving to be a very expensive business; and while he will make me a generous allowance after the ceremony, I am in need of funds, perhaps considerable funds, at present.'

'Your papa has made monies available to you already, Miss Fox,' the lawyer said, and Mariah quailed a little. He might keep a disorganised office, but Routledge was not going to be bullied by his client's daughter. 'Furthermore, I have put arrangements in place at several warehouses and with a Mademoiselle Juliette, modiste. Are these insufficient for your needs?'

'There has been an incident,' Mariah said, in dread of having to explain the Wellwoods' plot to him. As Mr Routledge's breathing became more laboured, an idea came to her. Was it not true to say that her papa's sudden collapse was an incident? 'Papa was taken ill this morning and a doctor was sent for. Naturally, Lord Mellon sent for the best doctor, and his bills will have to be met. As Papa is incapacitated, I have come to you to learn how much ready money can be realised from what he has set aside for my use and my dowry.'

'I have been in touch with the earl and his lawyers. Lord Mellon has offered to settle a generous jointure on you at the time of your nuptials, but it is customary for a young lady to take some money into her marriage where it is available. You would likely use it for your own daughters' portions and suchlike,' Routledge said quietly, and Mariah shifted in her seat. This was not proving as simple as matter as she had expected. She had not foreseen Mr Routledge taking such trouble to dissuade her. 'Your father would expect to deal with his own doctor's bills unless he is mentally incapacitated. Are you telling me that?'

Mariah was momentarily tempted to follow the suggestion, but Routledge could find out the truth of her father's condition so easily, she discarded the idea. How could she learn the sum of her entitlements? She believed it would be possible to bribe Lucas Wellwood. Surely, if he had ready cash, he would give up the plot over the tiara and leave Daisy alone? How much did a man of his nature regard as enough money?

'No sir, I am not telling you that. Papa is weakened in the body but not mentally. I need to know how much money I am able to raise from such resources as are set aside for me. If you please?' she asked, and studied the damaged reticule in her hands. Gazing up through her lashes she watched conflicting emotions flicker over Routledge's face, and tried to keep calm.

Did the man think she had been at the gaming tables? She read often enough in the newspapers how ladies of quality were tempted to bet as heavily as their husbands, and fortunes could be lost on the turn of a card. Did he think she had a shameful secret and was in need of funds to silence those who might share it? Perhaps he even thought it was something good like the endowment of a school? What did it matter what he thought? She needed access to the money if she was to defeat Lucas Wellwood.

'Mr Routledge?' she asked again, allowing just a touch of impatience to colour her tones.

'That is not an answer I can provide with any ease, Miss Fox,' the lawyer said. 'Your father's resources are complicated. Some family money in a trust, some rents. A certain amount is held in the funds. He has cash and inherited family artefacts. He has begun to address the question of how much he needs to keep for himself and how much he will make over to you now.' Mariah watched as Routledge stood up. 'In addition, of course, there is provision for Mrs Wilson to be factored. Your uncle is not a man of many means.'

'But he must have given you the idea of a figure to work towards, sir. What did you tell the earl's representatives?' Mariah asked, frustrated by his lack of co-operation. He clearly intended to fob her off with platitudes and visit her papa at the earliest opportunity.

'Three thousand pounds,' Routledge said finally. 'I am unhappy, Miss Fox. What is the incident that has caused you to make this visit?'

Mariah shook her head. She had never been distrusted before in her short life, and she did not enjoy the sensation. She would give anything to confide her woes in the lawyer, but the fewer people who knew of Wellwood's intentions, the better it must be. She would have to suffer Mr Routledge's disdain in silence.

'Very well, if you will not entrust your problem to me, I must hope that you have reached a sensible resolution of it. May I say that persons asking for funds to ensure their silence are rarely satisfied until the victim is bled white? When you become the Countess of Mellon, you will be an even more attractive prey, and at the mercy of whoever is doing this for years to come.'

'Mr Routledge,' Mariah began, but a vision of Daisy's sparkling brown eyes rose in her mind and quelled her instinct to seek advice. 'Mr Routledge, I will send my maid, Tilly, to you with a letter when I know how best to proceed. Thank you for seeing me today.'

12

Tobias towelled himself off after a hard bout of sparring at Mr Jackson's gymnasium. John, he thought grudgingly, had been right. There was nothing so good for clearing the mind as indulging in a quite different activity to thinking. Too much thinking, and one's brain only succeeded in creating ruts of worry where there should be flashes of brilliance.

His man handed him a clean linen shirt and waited with a fresh neck-cloth. Just as Tobias reached for that garment, he caught sight of Lucas Wellwood, and his hand stayed in mid-air. Perkins turned on the balls of his feet and let his gaze follow his master's. Tobias heard him say, 'Hurrumph.'

Pulling the neck-cloth into some semblance of style, Tobias thought for a moment or two. He'd already destroyed his credentials as a gentleman by hearing of Mariah's conversation. What else did he have to lose?

'What do you mean by that noise, Perkins? Is the noble baronet not to your taste?'

'My brother was in service with the late Lady Wellwood, your lordship,' Perkins said as he eased Tobias's tight-fitting coat across his shoulders. 'He told some tales about Sir Lucas. *And* the baronet was young at the time.'

'Headstrong, would your brother say?' Tobias asked.

'No sir, 'violent and evil' is what Rodney said. He left Lady Wellwood's employ when the second parlour-maid was found at the bottom of the service stair with her neck broken,' Perkins added. 'All the staff did, even Lady Wellwood's companion. This would have been while you were in France, my lord. As is the way with these matters . . . '

'It was hushed up,' Tobias interrupted. How easily the Wellwoods had fooled everyone. No doubt Lady Wellwood had produced satisfactory references in order to keep the departing staff silent. 'I don't think I need converse with Sir Lucas this afternoon, particularly as I must visit Miss Fox before I attend my mother this evening. While Lady Daisy is indisposed, it behoves me to escort Mama to a card party.'

*　*　*

Mariah heard the bell sound in the hall at Redde Place and waited for Josh to bring in a card. However, he was followed closely by Tobias, a Tobias whose face was unsmiling and whose deep brown gaze was filled with what might be called suspicion. Involuntarily, she turned to the fireplace where the red ribbon still lay curled among the kindling. How stupid. She had not thought Tobias would return today, and hadn't removed it.

He sat down across from her position

on the sofa without coming to place the now-customary kiss on her cheek. Mariah, whose state of agitation had hardly been lessened by her visit to the lawyer, lowered her gaze and waited.

'How does your papa do, Mariah?' Tobias asked, and she could have wept with relief. He had not found out about Amarinta's visit. He was simply subdued because he was worried about her papa.

'Well enough; although, as you will not be surprised to learn, he is sitting up in his chair and reading. And Daisy?' she asked in turn, casting an anxious look his way. Was Mr Routledge right? Would she spend the rest of her life worrying about whether Lucas Wellwood had succeeded in kidnapping her sister-in-law since the last time she saw her in person? Was this the way threats and blackmail worked?

'Eating buttered crumpets and driving the maids to distraction. However, my mother has refused to allow her to attend the card party this evening. I assume that *you* will wish to stay here while your papa is kept to his room?' Tobias crossed a booted leg over the other knee and Mariah was momentarily distracted. It was still a considerable thrill to be visited by a man in such fashionable dress. It was an even greater worry that his visits could cease at any time. Mariah realised how far she'd come from the modern educationalist with her eyes fixed on the one purpose of teaching the masses.

'Mariah?'

'I beg your pardon, Tobias. Yes, I will stay at home with Papa. I would wish to spend as much time as possible with him in the changed knowledge of his health,' she said diffidently. 'Will that be possible?'

'After we are married?' he asked, and considered the matter briefly. 'The society ladies are not falling over themselves with invitations as yet. We have been received only by those who know the family well, and wish to help my mama ease me back into the *ton*.

For the majority, I remain a subject of some suspicion. I'm afraid this tarnishes your name also, Mariah. Will you find it hard to forgo the glittering parties that might have been your entitlement?'

'Why, no. I am looking forward to our removal to your country house. Papa will feel the loss of his companions more than I, but perhaps your generosity in offering him a home might extend to inviting a couple of the closer among them to make extended visits. Besides, I have never regarded society as very important to my happiness.' She cast a questioning glance his way. He was in an odd humour, and she feared she had been too quick to judge herself free of enquiry. 'Daisy tells me there are several of the house servants and many of the estate workers with children. I will soon have a class in operation for them.'

'A class? Yes, that will serve well to keep you occupied — when I do not seek out your company, that is,' Tobias said, and Mariah could not ignore the challenge sparking in his eyes.

'Have I offended you in some way, sir?' she asked bluntly. 'Because I do not like the tone of your remark.'

'I use words though, Mariah,' he said, and rose to cross the room to the fire where he stooped and picked up the length of ribbon. 'Should you marry Sir Lucas, he might emphasise his points with his hands — or indeed a length of hazel, no thicker than his thumb.' He dropped the ribbon onto Mariah's clasped hands and stood over her.

'What nonsense is this? There has never been any question of my marrying Sir Lucas,' she said with fervour. 'This ribbon was tied around a letter his sister brought this morning.' She set it onto a side table, loath to have it brushing her skin. 'She came to wish me well in my marriage, and to acquaint me of the details of her own.'

She heard Tobias's sharp intake of breath. How easy it was to twist the truth just enough to make the other person seem to be in the wrong, but she could not meet his glance.

'Amarinta came here to wish you well?' he asked, and Mariah heard the utter disbelief. Perhaps not so easy to lie as she had thought. 'Mariah, we should not start our married life with secrets between us. You are lying on that one point, if nothing else.'

Mariah felt his hands grip her elbows and he pulled her onto her feet. He was so close his breath fanned her hair. Her thoughts were in turmoil. Had one of the servants given something away about the trip to Mr Routledge's?

'Surely you would not expect me to blacken the lady's name by complaining of her behaviour, particularly when she had thought to be a candidate for your hand herself?' she said quietly. The doorbell clanged once more in the hall, but she was very little aware of it. Mariah knew this was an opportunity to apprise Tobias of her troubles, but she was unsure how to do it. She drew a deep breath while she collected her thoughts, but was startled by Josh's interruption.

'Miss Mariah,' the boy said, and stepped forward to present his tray, which held a visiting card with a distinctive oak tree embossed across one corner.

'Wellwood,' Tobias said. 'I recognise his cipher.' He ground the name between his teeth like a distasteful piece of gristle. 'How does Sir Lucas think to visit here?'

Mariah blushed in confusion. Why did Sir Lucas visit here? She took his card and turned it in her fingers to find a message scrawled on the back in thin spidery letters.

'Apparently, he sends his good wishes for my papa's health; and on discovering that you are present, would like to present them in person,' she said, reading the cramped sentences quickly. She handed the card to Tobias so he might see for himself.

Tobias scanned the words and tossed

the card onto the salver. He spoke directly to Josh.

'Tell Sir Lucas that Miss Fox is receiving no one in the circumstances,' he said in clipped tones.

'Tobias . . . ' Mariah began, but was quelled into silence by the simmering anger of her betrothed. She knew he could think of no reason why she should allow a visit from another man outside her family. She brought her hand nervously up to her face and thought how best to go on. There was no doubt she wished Lucas Wellwood anywhere but here. On the other hand, if he did not have an audience with her now, would he come back when she was unprotected? 'You are of course right, Tobias, but I think it would be best if he were admitted. Show the baronet in please, Josh.'

'Your lordship?' Josh asked, and Mariah had to bite back the protest that rose at this questioning of her authority. It was her house but Josh was Tobias's servant. Tobias's eyes held her gaze and she had to force herself to keep her head high, as she had practised when teaching bigger boys who didn't want to learn and were set on causing disruption. Whatever Tobias saw in her troubled blue gaze must have persuaded him to accede to her wishes.

'Yes, Josh, show him in,' he said.

They waited in silence. Mariah thought of the grim picture Amarinta had painted of the life of any woman Lucas might marry. She visualised the girl's pride as she had protested to Mariah that Lucas was a concerned guardian. Would Daisy be reduced to such straits if the worst happened? She had to fool him into believing she would accede to his monstrous demands while she forced Mr Routledge to release her three thousand pounds.

Sir Lucas was fully into the room, and they had all made polite bows and assumed seats before Mariah saw the length of red ribbon from Amarinta's letter again. Tobias had retrieved it from her side table and was twining it around his fingers. Within seconds, it had drawn Sir Lucas's attention, and his dark features closed in to make his face a mask of chiselled fury.

Tobias knew. Mariah's spirits plummeted further even than they had fallen in the course of this dreadful day. Josh was a spy. The thoughts tumbled around in her head until she felt as if it would explode. The earl had come here to give her the chance to explain, and she had not taken it. Now, with Lucas Wellwood sitting in her morning room on the thinnest of excuses, it must look to him as if she was in collusion with the baronet.

★ ★ ★

Tobias waited. Mariah had had a chance to tell him about the extraordinary missive she had received. She could have explained how it was a plot of Wellwood's. She could have said she'd been coming to him and John

Brent to tell them.

He twisted the ribbon through his long fingers and gauged the effect his actions were having on the two others in the room. Mariah was agitated and, if she were made of less stern stuff, would have collapsed in a faint. Wellwood was so angry he was finding it difficult to contain the emotion. Tobias fancied that in more familiar company he would have let off an explosion of wrath by now.

'I believe I caught sight of you at Jackson's rooms earlier, Mellon,' Wellwood said. 'I had some talk with your sparring partner, Linklater, and discovered that Miss Fox's papa had been taken ill and that you would be making your way here. So I decided to follow on and ask after the invalid.' He turned his hooded gaze toward Mariah and Tobias watched the encounter closely. Did she attempt to send any signals towards the man? 'How does your esteemed papa go on, Miss Fox?'

'He is comfortable, thank you, Sir

Lucas. He reads and has taken a small meal,' Mariah replied without any warmth.

'I am most relieved to learn that. I congratulate you,' Wellwood said.

'No congratulation is required for my actions, sir. It was all down to Doctor Moon.' Mariah spoke with a catch in her voice and Tobias saw a glimmer of sparkle in her eyes.

'Does the good doctor believe it will be necessary to delay your nuptials?' Wellwood asked, and Tobias understood why he had come. His finances must be in a very dire way to prompt him to make such an unconventional visit.

'It is kind of you to exhibit such concern, Wellwood. However, no final decision has been taken. Miss Fox wishes to see how her papa copes with his new regime,' Tobias said, while smoothing the ribbon through his fingers and letting it fall in a stream of rippling red. Had it been the rag of proverb, Wellwood would have called him out by now on any pretext.

'I see,' Wellwood said. 'Miss Fox will have many considerations to bring to bear on her decision.'

'I do,' Mariah said, 'and while it was good of you to pay your respects in person, Sir Lucas, I am afraid I must ask you to cut short your visit. It has been a long and tiring day.'

Tobias watched as Wellwood rose to his feet. He fixed the full strength of his dark gaze on Mariah but she did not drop hers. The baronet made a small bow to them both and turned to the door where Josh stood half-in, half-out of the room. How long had the boy been standing there? Wellwood had not found any welcome in this house, he thought, with a degree of satisfaction. Nonetheless, Josh was no match for the evil that Wellwood commanded. He would send a couple of the burlier footmen from Grosvenor Square to augment his efforts.

* * *

Mariah waited for the door to close behind their unwanted visitor before she dared to look at her betrothed. He raised an eyebrow and she knew the time for stalling was over.

'You know what was in the letter Amarinta brought here this morning,' she said, 'and so you must think I was planning to collude with Sir Lucas Wellwood to rob you and your family.'

'No, Mariah. I do not think that. I spent a very uncomfortable couple of hours puzzling over why you would receive such a letter and not take me into your confidence, but John Brent has helped me to see the matter from your point of view.' She watched as Tobias crossed to the table that held some freshly-replenished decanters. He poured a glass of ratafia for her and took some brandy.

'I am not used to anything as strong, and . . .'

'I think it will steady your nerves, which are clearly a little overset by so many untoward events,' Tobias said brusquely, but there was no kindness in his voice. Her heart ached for his smile.

'It is so much worse than you imagine, Tobias,' she said at last. 'Sir Lucas expected you to marry his sister because no-one else would accept your hand after Leo died. The plan to steal the tiara was then thought up, and when he was flush from gaming, he had a copy made.'

'You learned all this from Amarinta?' Tobias asked, and she nodded. 'But that much John and I were able to work out. What I am unable to see is why you did not tell me. I was deeply upset and very worried by your lack of trust. Do you never have regard for consequences?'

'You are unkind, sir, to bring such a charge up when I have been frantic with worry,' she said. Her protest did nothing to ease Tobias's anger, and he waited for her to explain further. 'Sir Lucas has long had a wish to marry Lady Daisy, although he knows you would never permit it.'

'Permit it? After what I've learned

about the man recently, I would kill him first,' Tobias said vehemently. Glancing at the expression marring his strong-boned face, Mariah had no hesitation in believing him.

'He has formed a back-up plan. If I do not co-operate with his instructions, he will abduct Daisy and, and . . . ' Mariah found it impossible to utter the words, and Tobias had to rescue her from the horror.

'Force a marriage in the manner of the desperate fortune hunter,' he said.

Mariah quailed. She had found him forbidding before. He was now quite terrifying in his anger.

She raised the glass of ratafia and swallowed it in one. The sweet liqueur burned a fiery trail down her throat and caused her eyes to water.

'Tobias,' she said. 'I have a plan.'

'Do you? Would that have anything to do with your absence from this house for two hours in the company of only your maid?'

'We will not do together if you insist

on allowing Josh to spy on me,' Mariah protested. 'He must have told you I received Amarinta and that I was going to visit Daisy, which of course, you know I didn't.' The words were a little petulant but her head felt different, odd. It was a great effort to keep her eyes focussed.

'How else can I discover what you are getting up to? I gave you ample opportunity to tell me about the letter . . .'

'But you'd heard what it contained. Not exactly the action of a gentleman,' she said. Oh dear, she thought, as Tobias studied her with the kind of glare that must have had his soldiers quaking. She should not have said that.

'Did you eat anything before you went off on this wild goose chase, Mariah?' he asked in an apparently random sally.

'Eat something? Do you think that is why I am feeling a little tired? Usually I have a good appetite, but today I was unable to face any luncheon,' she said.

Tobias was looking at her very intently and she thought he muttered an oath, but surely she was mistaken. Tobias *was* a gentleman. He would never use such language in her hearing.

'It is too bad that you are concerned only with my behaviour. You do not ask about my plan,' she said, hiccupping, 'which I believe is a good one.'

In fact, she was beginning to have doubts about it. Three thousand pounds had seemed such an enormous amount of money, but when she began to recall the kind of sums Daisy spent on her modiste and her milliner, she was less confident that it would tempt Sir Lucas away from his objective. Not only did he have to dress himself, he had an estate to maintain and servants to pay. Perhaps she had been too ready to believe he would fall in with her offer because it was so important to her that he should.

'How much money does a man in Sir Lucas's position need to maintain his life?' she asked. There was no point in dismissing her idea without establishing the full facts.

'More, much more than you could lay hands on, even if you persuaded your papa to sell everything he owns,' Tobias said. 'I have had a note from Mr Routledge.'

'You have?' she asked, feeling defeated.

'Wellwood has debts that you cannot even begin to fathom. Really, Mariah, I begin to wonder if Peter Sharp did not have the right of things.'

'What things?' she asked, and her brain was less fuddled than it had been. How could she marry him if he thought like Peter Sharp?

'Things like a female being unable to enter fully into the results of her thoughtless and self-centred actions,' he said.

'I see, my lord, that your conversion to the benefits of education for women has been short-lived. Perhaps you will find that there is no space in my day or any room in your vast house for me to hold a class once we are married? Or, worse, that only the male children may be taught their letters,' she said and was gratified by the embarrassed blush that stained his cheek.

'Do not think to manipulate me, Mariah,' he said. He crossed to the bell-pull, tugging it brutally. 'I think you should have a little food and lie down.'

'I am not yet under your jurisdiction, Tobias. You cannot order me around,' she said, as she stood up to better make her point. Unfortunately, standing was like being on the deck of a ship. The floor was not quite as steady as it had been earlier, and while her head no longer felt fuzzy and her thoughts were clear, she would be glad to put her hand onto the back of a chair. Only she missed the chair and found herself pitching forward.

'I should have listened to you,' Tobias said as he caught her and slid an arm beneath her knees to lift her against his chest. 'You are not used to ratafia.'

'Put me down,' she protested.

'I think not. There you are Tilly,' he said as the maid entered the room. 'Your mistress is in need of some food and rest.'

Mariah closed her eyes in despair. Before Tobias had reached the upper floor, she was falling into sleep. His setting her down on the counterpane, and running his hand tenderly along her cheek to hold her chin in long fingers, was the start of a troubling dream.

13

Tobias powered up the central staircase in Grosvenor Square toward his mother's rooms. He could not accompany her to the card party in view of the information he'd gleaned from Mariah before she passed out in his arms. Silly chit, he thought, although when he remembered her accusation that he had not behaved like a gentleman, his indulgent smile became strained.

Two weeks and four days until he would be able to have her entirely to himself. In the solitude of the marriage bed, he would teach her so many things her questing intelligence had no knowledge of at present. The thought acted as balm to his troubled spirits, but Wellwood and the risks he represented could not be allowed to languish. He had to get hold of John Brent and one or two other trusted friends, and act immediately. When they were successful, his marriage to Mariah would be his reward.

'Mama, I regret that I am unable to accompany you this evening,' he said to Constanzia when he reached her suite. 'There is a matter of business that won't wait.'

'Business? What business, Tobias?' Constanzia asked. She was closeted with her dressmaker and Anna, poring over journals of ladies' fashions. 'What business is more important than taking care of your parent?'

'I know it is difficult to imagine that playing whist with twenty ladies of your acquaintance is not sufficient enticement from the mundane, but I regret it is so,' he said, and tempered the remark with the kind of devastating smile only mothers and their sons understood.

'Very well,' Constanzia agreed. 'I think you take some delight in frustrating my efforts to secure you a welcome in Society. I would have a word in private with you. Please allow us a moment, ladies?'

Tobias held the door for Anna and the dressmaker to leave and then turned a questioning glance toward his mama. She had become quiet and he feared the worst.

'Have you changed your mind about your journey to Spain, Mama?' he asked. 'Has my cousin backed out of his promise to accompany you?'

'No, I have not changed my mind, and Henry Menzies will travel with us. No, Tobias, it is Daisy I am concerned about. She has told me that Sir Lucas Wellwood has begun to single her out at events and has sent her flowers on more than one occasion. I cannot like it. If I have been incensed by mutterings among the *ton* about your part in Leo's death, then I should be disposed to disregard anything said about Sir Lucas as similar gossip. However, I find I cannot,' she said, letting the journal in her hand slip from her grasp.

'Calm yourself, Mama, Daisy has done the correct thing in confiding her fears to you. There is no cause to worry,' Tobias lied without shame. 'I am aware Wellwood's finances are in a dire state, and I will take every care to prevent him securing an interview with Daisy. She is no longer an intimate of Miss Wellwood.'

'I am of the belief that Amarinta Wellwood sought me out and cultivated my good opinion in order to have me champion her in your eyes. Which I feel I did, much to my chagrin.' The countess pleated the silk of her gown. 'Tobias, what *did* happen?'

Tobias did not pretend to misunderstand his mother, but replied simply, 'Leo took the sheath off the tip of my blade while he distracted our attention by fidgeting with his jerkin. None of us realised until he sustained the injury. It was bad luck that it turned septic, of course, because the wound itself was not deep enough or positioned to cause his death.'

'I have always suspected as much. It is the reason I have raised no objection to your alliance with Mariah Fox. She is well-born enough, but her intelligence must be viewed as a considerable handicap to marital harmony,' Constanzia said. 'However, she is your choice, and you have suffered much because of Leo. I will make her welcome into the family.'

'Thank you, Mama. I must tell you that John Brent came to me earlier and asked my permission to address Daisy with a view to marrying her. Will you also welcome him? His finances have been restored by the discovery of coal under his land in the Northeast.'

'Coal! One must assume that he does not intend to hew this stuff himself?'

'There was much talk of managers and mining engineers. I cannot think Daisy will be required to wash moleskin trousers,' Tobias said with a smile.

'No, but I wonder whether she needs something to occupy her beyond the round of the Season. She has been much enchanted by Miss Fox and her class teaching,' she said, and sighed.

'This will become Mr Brent's problem, and he has sisters in plenty so he will know how to go on.'

'He has,' Tobias agreed.

'I will stay at home this evening. I cannot be other than nervous about Wellwood, and I do not wish to leave Daisy alone in the house,' the countess said, and Tobias was relieved.

'Thank you, Mama. I have sent a couple of footmen along to Redde Place and alerted the staff that neither Wellwood nor his sister should be admitted there. Stephens is aware, too, so there should be no problem here.'

His mother studied him and, too late, he realised that he had given away the nature of his *mundane* business.

'I hope you will act sensibly, Tobias. I have lost one son and have no desire to lose another,' she said finally. Tobias bowed over her hand and left. There was little he could say to ease her agitation. Wellwood had thrown down a gauntlet when he had his sister deliver the letter. Tobias had picked it up when he sat twining that ribbon around his fingers.

He might easily avoid duelling with the likes of Peter Sharp, but he could not compromise his honour by ignoring Wellwood. No, he thought, the man must be met, but it need not lead to the death of one or the other. His brain had enjoyed military tactics when he was in the army, and he was forming plans as he rang for Perkins. Before he set off for his club to hunt out Brent and one or two friends, he needed to find out where Perkins' brother Rodney could be located. It seemed wise to learn all that could be gleaned about the late Lady Wellwood's dead parlour-maid.

While he waited for his man to answer the summons, he wondered what Mariah's plan might have been. It niggled that she had not come straight to him with Wellwood's proposal. Perhaps she had been allowed too much licence by her papa. However much he hoped to let her continue with teaching and assisting others to teach, there were constraints in life. She seemed to think ignoring them would erase them.

She would now leave the matter of Wellwood for him to sort out, wouldn't she? If he were a betting man, he would not accept odds on that. Just as well, he thought, that Josh knew where his first loyalty lay.

*　*　*

Mariah woke, and lay for several minutes in the daylight gloom of her bedroom. She heard Tilly singing on the landing, and children screaming at their games in the communal garden behind the house, so she knew it could not be very late.

She hauled herself up the bed and rested against the bank of pillows. What must Tobias think of her? The honest answer to that question was too embarrassing for her to contemplate, so she took refuge in righteous anger. How dare he make her drink ratafia when she was unaccustomed to more than a token sip of champagne at evening functions? How dare he dismiss her plan to see off Sir Lucas without even hearing what it was? Didn't he realise how dangerous the man was?

Questions tumbled through her mind and answers did not come easily. Yet one thing was very clear to Mariah before she had consumed the meal Tilly brought to her on a tray. Amarinta Wellwood was in danger immediately. Wellwood had seen that the girl had followed his instructions by leaving the letter, but he had also seen that the earl knew what was in the missive.

Mariah felt a dark dread growing in her stomach when she thought of Wellwood and his unbridled passions. He must already have worked out that she had told Tobias of the threat to Daisy he had used as blackmail. It was very likely that he would twist this failure of his plans in his mind, and blame his sister for it.

He would know that Tobias would

engage men to protect Daisy. Mr Barlow would not know that he needed to guard his bride from her own brother. But then, she reminded herself, Amarinta did not want Reginald or his mama to know that he was marrying a woman whose brother was about to drag the family into scandal by association.

The ramifications of sending notes to one or the other, or of trying to seek a meeting with Amarinta or Lady Barlow, danced in her head until she was on the point of screaming. How did one resolve this?

'Begging your pardon, Miss Mariah, but you're like a cat on a skillet,' Tilly said as she tried to brush out her mistress's hair. 'I know it was unfortunate to fall asleep on the earl an' all, but he'll get over it.'

'That's not what's causing my anxiety, Tilly.' There was no prospect of keeping any secrets from Tilly now that they spent so much time in each other's company. 'I am very disturbed by the possible revenge Sir Lucas Wellwood will exact over the failure of his plans.'

'No need, miss. The earl has sent two very large footmen along from Grosvenor Square. He's ordered one to sleep across the garden door and one in the front hall. Josh is to bed down in the morning room,' Tilly said.

Mariah groaned.

'What's the matter? Isn't that a good plan?'

'It means I won't be able to go out without them alerting the earl,' she said. It had not occurred to her that Tobias thought *she* was in any danger. Why would Wellwood seek her out when she was betrothed and worth a measly three thousand pounds?

'He's given instructions that you aren't to go out at all until his say-so changes them instructions,' Tilly said.

Mariah's storm-filled eyes met her maid's in the mirror. 'He's done what?' she asked, jumping to her feet.

'And I agree with him, miss,' Tilly said quietly. 'The servants that come in and out of here from Grosvenor Square know what's what, they do.'

'Meaning?'

'Sir Lucas Wellwood is thought to be a man with blood on his hands, miss. Female blood, not respectable like in a duel or something.' The girl bent to lift the stool Mariah had overturned. 'There's a strong rumour that he threw a parlour-maid down some stairs and broke her neck.'

'Exactly,' Mariah said vehemently. 'I must get to his sister before Sir Lucas does, to warn her that their plans to rob the Mellon family have failed. To tell her the earl knows of *all* their plans.'

'It's over two hours since Sir Lucas left, miss. Won't he have gone straight home?'

'How does one know what gentlemen do?' Mariah asked in turn. How did she know what Tobias was doing? She had a very clear memory of his anger and of Wellwood's. Had they been younger men, there would already be arrangements for a duel in place. Tobias had told her he did not call men out — but how could he do otherwise, when he had discovered Wellwood embroiled in plans to steal his family jewels and abduct his sister? He might also be in added danger, because she was sure Wellwood would not fight fairly.

'Begging your pardon, miss, but why would you be wanting to warn someone who had tried to rob the earl?' Tilly asked diffidently.

'Because she is not the instigator of these things, and because Wellwood will blame her for the failure of his schemes and take revenge on her,' Mariah said. 'Would you have me stand aside? Should I wait until her lifeless body is found and some servant brought to book for the death?'

Tilly dropped the hairbrush and gaped. She lifted a hand to her throat, and as Mariah watched, the girl struggled to breathe, becoming red in the face.

'Tilly, what is the matter?' She pushed the maid gently onto a stool.

'It's not right that women are afraid in their own homes, miss. I was overcome,' the girl said when she had recovered a little.

'Were the women afraid in your family home?' Mariah asked. Tilly only ever spoke of females. No father or brother appeared in the tales of her crowded household.

'Perhaps they were,' she said, but would not meet Mariah's eyes. Her hands bunched the cotton material of her skirts and worked it so hard Mariah thought her thighs would be bruised beneath. 'Perhaps we wasn't as sad as we might be when my dad fell in the Thames, too drunk to 'aul 'isself out. Perhaps we encouraged George and Matthew to enlist, an' didn't miss them when they run off to the Peninsula.'

Mariah put her arms around the girl and hugged her. It caused Tilly to burst into loud tears. Her frame was thin, shaking and vulnerable, just as Amarinta's might be at this moment. Mariah knew she had to do something, but how could she ask Tilly to help when she was so overwhelmed by the thoughts of her family?

'I am so sorry to learn this about your early life, Tilly. I think you should take the rest of today off and go to visit your mother,' Mariah said.

Tilly leapt up from the stool and shook down her dress. She rubbed the back of her hand across her eyes and wiped the tears away. 'Oh no, Miss Mariah, if you can risk the earl's good regard an' all to help Miss Wellwood, then I ain't leaving you to do it alone. How would you get out of this house without me to distract them oafs the earl has sent along?'

'Thank you, Tilly. There may be a little danger in this plan, but we will take every care.'

'Do you know where Miss Wellwood lives, miss?'

'Yes, Lady Daisy mentioned the name of the street when she was talking one day. It is called Ogle Road. She also said it was a tall, thin house, with balconies below the windows on the first floor. We must hope that only one or two houses are adorned with balconies,' Mariah said. In truth, Tilly had a good point, because the earl had scrunched Wellwood's card into his pocket. Mariah thought the house number written there might have been fourteen, but she had been agitated. It could equally have been four or twenty-four.

'Ogle Road,' Tilly said. 'My sisters did not allow me to go for interview to any families in that area when I was starting out. Should we take Josh with us, miss?'

'Josh is loyal to his master and would prevent our expedition. I think we have to rely on our wits alone. I will understand, Tilly, if you feel it is too dangerous.'

'No, miss, I won't let you down. How are we to get you out of the house?'

★ ★ ★

Across town, Tobias and John Brent, with Linklater and a fourth friend called Goreton, ate an early dinner in White's. They had tossed ideas among themselves and had come to a resolution on how to proceed. They first needed to contact Rodney Perkins and bring him to Wellwood's residence.

'I'll go now,' Linklater said, as he stood up and cast his eyes around the room. 'There's that encroaching fellow who's going to marry Miss Wellwood. Gawd, if he isn't coming this way. Would you like me to head him off, Toby?'

'Encroaching because his money comes from trade, eh, Links?' Brent asked, flushing slightly.

'No, John. Don't mount your high horse with me. I couldn't be more pleased for you that your ground's got coal. No, it's his manner. Too late, you're about to find out for yourself. I'm on my way. Coming, Goreton?' Linklater addressed the men in turn, and Tobias saw his small smile as

Goreton hacked off a final piece of beefsteak to stuff into his mouth before he rose to follow on.

A shadow replaced the departing friends, and Tobias glanced up to see Reginald Barlow looming. The young man was large, and his skin was pasty in a manner that reminded Tobias of many of his soldiers. Was he consumptive?

'My lord,' Barlow said, and made a ponderous bow. 'Mr Brent, I believe,' he added, including John in his address. 'I hope you will forgive this intrusion. I felt it incumbent — despite finding you, your lordship, in the company of men who have every appearance of being your very good friends — to come over and make something known to you.'

Tobias was in a quandary. They had not been introduced, but the young man was oblivious to his social solecism, or perhaps not and ignoring it. Whatever the reason for his eccentric behaviour, he was loud. If he had anything to say about Amarinta Wellwood, then Tobias and John needed to hear it, but it would be infinitely preferable that the rest of the evening company in the club did not. He stood up and invited Barlow to join them at the table.

'You are very gracious, your lordship. I am not unaware,' he said, and looked squarely at John Brent, 'that I should have engineered an introduction, but my business would not wait.'

'Please do not trouble yourself on that head, sir,' Tobias said, and John acknowledged the young man with a quick nod that might pass for a bow. 'In what way may I be of service to you?'

'I think it is rather I who might be of service to you. As you may know I am to marry Miss Amarinta Wellwood by special licence the day after tomorrow. When I called at her home this afternoon, I found a loud altercation going forward. In any other establishment, the servant would not have allowed me across the threshold, but it is very ramshackle there,' Barlow said. 'Why, only last week there was an actual fight taking place in one of the rooms. I heard glass breaking and furniture crashing.'

'Today,' John asked, 'did it appear to be an argument between members of the household?'

'Between my betrothed and her brother, in fact,' Barlow confirmed. 'I overheard your name, Lord Mellon, and in subsequent discussion, Miss Wellwood has made some information known to me. This is why I have sought you out.'

'Is Miss Wellwood safe?' Tobias asked.

'Yes,' the younger man said, and he narrowed his gaze. 'I will not ask why you use that word. If I do not know what earlier shadows hang over the family, then I will not unwittingly reveal them to my mama. I take the view that the less my mama knows about Miss Wellwood's brother before the wedding, the greater the chances of it taking place as arranged,' Barlow said calmly. 'I have taken Miss Wellwood to my grandmother's house and left several men in and around it. Sir Lucas Wellwood will not see his sister again, if I have anything to do with it.'

'And the information Miss Wellwood made known to you?' Tobias prompted as Barlow puffed out his chest, apparently reflecting on how clever he had been in rescuing his betrothed.

'I regret to have to tell you that the scoundrel has set in motion plans to abduct your sister, my lord. They would follow on from the failure of his plans to steal a tiara from your betrothed on her wedding morning. I could not make any sense of that, as I know Mr Jerome Fox by reputation. The reputation does not lead one to expect tiaras in the cupboard,' Barlow concluded.

'I don't suppose Miss Wellwood gleaned any details of the proposed abduction?' Tobias ventured. Unwilling to allow Miss Fox's part in these matters to be voiced, he did not enlighten Barlow about the tiara's ownership. The man would no doubt hear all from Amarinta in due course.

'No, my lord. Indeed, Wellwood was screaming how it was as well that he hadn't entrusted her with such details when I interrupted. I told him he would hear from my friends. I am a passable shot, you must know, and can handle the sword when necessary, but he said he would not consider meeting anyone who was not a gentleman. Furthermore, he announced that if I wanted to marry his sister, I would have to pay him twenty thousand pounds.'

'You threatened to call him out because he wouldn't tell his sister some details?' John asked incredulously.

The young man's eyes became pinpoints of fury and he stood up. 'No, sir. I wished to call him out because he backed up his harangue with a blow to Miss Wellwood's head.' He bowed to both men and left as abruptly as he had arrived.

Tobias and John sat in silence for a moment or two. It was shocking indeed to hear Barlow describe Wellwood's treatment of the sister who lived solely in his care and depended entirely on his whim.

Had Mariah known of this? he wondered. The night they encountered the baronet in Lady Melchambers's house, Mariah had been very quiet when he returned with their refreshment. She had fobbed him off, he now thought. What if she knew how Wellwood went on in his home? Would she be moved to intervene on Amarinta's behalf?

'So Amarinta Wellwood is worth twenty thousand pounds?' John said, in an attempt at nervous humour.

'She is twenty-two years old, John, and free to marry as she chooses. I do not see our Northern mill owner paying her brother anything except a bloody nose, should he get the chance,' Tobias said.

'Yes, indeed. He loves her,' John said. 'It is remarkable.'

'That a mill owner should have feelings?'

'No, Toby, I am not such a high-in-the-instep stickler as you would make me out. No, sadly perhaps, I have always found Miss Wellwood to be a most unlovable young woman.'

'Perhaps her brother's treatment is responsible for that,' Tobias said thoughtfully. 'If we have come to this conclusion, how will Miss Fox be regarding the relations between brother and sister?'

'Females are always quicker to make such observations,' John agreed. 'You are worried that Miss Fox may circumvent your arrangements to keep her safely inside the Redde Place house. If she believes she needs to rescue Miss Wellwood from her brother's viciousness, she may try to evade Josh and the extra footmen.'

Tobias was already on his feet and heading for the door. 'I think we will go straight to Ogle Road,' he called back over his shoulder as John gathered their scattered belongings. 'I think Miss Fox's quick understanding will lead her to attempt to escape, and I am afraid

297

she will probably succeed.'

Mariah, Tobias thought, please do not make another rash decision. Please do not concoct a plan to beard Wellwood in his own home.

14

Mariah sat in the morning room. Josh, who had been detailed to sleep in that room later, was about his business in the house at present. She had heard him knock and enter her papa's room on the first floor.

In due course, Tilly came in. Mariah rose to assist her with the huge bundle of wedding clothes she was carrying. They shut the door onto the hall.

'He's a big brute, and no mistake.' Tilly nodded toward the hall where one of Tobias's footmen sat or paced the hours away. 'I don't reckon Sir Lucas would have much success getting past him.'

'It is likely Sir Lucas will have someone similar holding his front door inviolable,' Mariah replied. 'Although one must hope not. Do you have my boots?'

'Yes, miss, and some for myself.' She slid her bundle onto a table-top and eased the boots out of it. Two spencers were also hidden in the pile. 'There's no bonnet,' Tilly wailed. 'How can you be seen on the street without a bonnet?'

'I have one across by the fireplace. I did not give it to you when we returned from the visit to Mr Routledge,' Mariah said, and quickly retrieved it. The women changed into walking clothes and crossed toward the doors that opened onto the garden. Mariah gripped the handle, but the door was locked. She reached for the key to turn it, but found the keyhole empty.

Together, they searched around the floor and checked shelves and the drawers of the desks but it was no use. Tobias had clearly given instructions to Josh, and Josh had followed them. The key was gone.

'He intends to hold me prisoner,' Mariah said.

'He intends to keep you safe, Miss,' Tilly corrected. 'Not but what it ain't a nuisance, and no mistake, 'cos it is an' all.'

'There is no lock on the window, Tilly,' Mariah said, and they both looked at a small window set into the back wall beside the bigger glazed doors. Below it, outside, there was a trough full of night-scented stock, but it was not very far above ground. If they could squeeze through, they would not have far to slide out onto the back area, Mariah thought. 'It had bars at one time,' she said as she removed her boots, 'but Papa had them removed when one of the boot-boys injured his eye trying to prise them apart to let his sweetheart in.'

She saw what Tilly thought of that story without asking, and busied herself moving a sturdy chair below the window. It would be too bad if one of them got stuck in the window-frame. She must not allow defeat to creep into her thoughts. Amarinta's life might depend on whether they were able to escape Tobias's arrangements.

'I will go first because I am bigger than you and I would not expect you to go alone. If I can get through, then so will you,' Mariah said, and stuck her head out of the window.

Within minutes she was scrabbling out of the trough of flowers and trying not to cry out. Her legs were scraped from contact with the window frame and her dress was torn in two or three places. She took two pairs of boots from Tilly and both their reticules, together with her bonnet. Tilly soon tumbled into the flowers to join her.

'Pull the window back into place, miss,' Tilly advised. 'Then they won't feel a draught in the hall. We should have twenty minutes before Letty from Grosvenor Square wants to set light to the kindling.'

'That's done,' Mariah said. 'Now, there is an entrance to the central park area between the corner houses across there.' She pointed toward the east side of the communal area. 'It will bring us out most conveniently. We will not have to retrace our steps past the windows of Redde Place.'

* * *

Tobias leapt from the hackney he and John Brent had used to travel to Wellwood's rented house in Ogle Road. His face was wet with perspiration and blood thundered in his ears. What if they were too late and Mariah, darling misguided Mariah, had succeeded in arriving before them? It was too dire to contemplate.

'The front door is ajar,' John said, and grabbed one of Tobias's arms from behind. 'No, don't fight with me, man. We must move with some stealth. Wait for us,' he called to the driver of the hackney, and tossed up a few coins as a marker of good faith.

Tobias shook free from John's hold, but stayed his step. His friend was right, and he must think as a trained soldier, not as a besotted lover.

Sir Lucas may already have engaged

thugs to help in his planned abduction of Daisy, Tobias thought. *If so, then they could be lurking on the premises waiting to accost any unwelcome callers. John and I will be of no use to Mariah if we're unconscious or trussed like pigs going to market.* He shuddered.

'You sent another hackney to bring Linklater and Goreton here, whether they have found Perkins' brother or not,' John reminded him urgently. 'We should wait until they arrive.'

'No, John. I cannot stand by when Mariah might be in there and in danger,' Tobias hissed. 'We must find a way in, by-passing the front entrance.'

They had crossed the flagstones and were surveying a building of little charm. It rose above them to three stories from an outside staircase. The windows on the first floor were tall and opened onto small iron balconies. The architect may have thought he was giving the whole an appearance of grandeur by his design, but somehow it had been missed in the execution. A shop selling bolts of cloth occupied the ground floor and was entered directly from the street, but there was no activity and the owner had probably closed up for the night.

'Let's try down the entry,' John said. 'It slopes upwards, and so the windows at the back may enter the house and not the shop.'

They set off into the dark passageway down the side of the building, and had not gone very far when they heard a female groaning. Shadows moved, letting the men see where the woman lay, but suspecting a trap, they stopped.

'Who's there?' Tobias asked. 'Identify yourself.'

'Is that you, your lordship?' Tilly asked. Her voice was weak and her breathing came in short gasps. 'Oh, your lordship, he's got her.'

'Mariah?' Tobias breathed the name. 'Who's got her, Tilly?'

'The devil, sir. The very devil,' Tilly said bleakly.

'Why, it's Miss Fox's maid,' Brent said. 'Do you mean Wellwood, missy?' He moved forward and began to assist Tilly off her knees. 'What's this?' he asked as his hand made contact with her arms. 'Are you bleeding?'

'Tilly?' Tobias said, 'Have they harmed you?' Together, the men eased Tilly onto her feet, and helped her move along the passageway back toward the street. As soon as they were into the light, they could see that Tilly had sustained a head injury. Copious amounts of blood soaked into her spencer and matted her hair.

'The fiend!' Brent said as Tilly's legs gave way and she sank toward the flagstones. Sliding his arm under her knees, John looked around for somewhere to place her safely.

'The hackney, man!' Tobias shouted. 'We're going in. We cannot wait for the others.'

Tobias cleared the short flight of steps in two bounds and leapt into the house's hallway. There was little light, and he had to slow down lest he collide with something in the gloom. It was quiet. It was unnaturally quiet. Tobias stopped and listened.

Brent came up the outside stair and Tobias heard him halt in the doorway. The noises of the street filtered in. Horses clipped along, men hailed one another. Inside this unprepossessing house nothing made a sound.

Except . . . Tobias cocked his head. There was a noise. It was rhythmic. It was a noise he recognised. It was the noise prisoners made when they rubbed their bindings against a sharp edge in the hope of securing their release. His heart soared. She was here. For whatever reason, Wellwood had left her here a captive.

Gesturing behind him to keep Brent quiet, Tobias padded along the carpet in even steps. He passed a door on his right and kept on toward the back of the hallway. The noise increased to a crescendo.

Tobias threw open the final door in

the passage just as Mariah split the strip of cotton securing her wrists and tying her to a chair. A slender piece of glass fell to the floor.

'Mariah.' Tobias rushed forward to release the gag that had prevented her crying out. 'Darling girl, are you unharmed?' he asked as his eyes scoured her for signs that Wellwood or his men had coshed her, too.

'Tilly,' she said as soon as she could form words. 'Have you found her, Tobias? They hit her over the head and I fear the worst.'

'Yes, she is alive, although she has lost a lot of blood and was fainting when I saw her last,' Tobias said. 'Are you unharmed, Mariah?' he asked again. His fingers unravelled the remainder of the cotton strips tying her to the chair.

'I am unharmed,' she replied. 'Please, Tobias, let us leave this house. It has a repressive atmosphere.'

Brent crashed forward into the room, banging against Tobias before catching his temple against the corner of a table.

Tobias and Mariah turned startled gazes over Brent's prone form towards the door.

'A fine collection of trespassers.' Wellwood's nasal sneer cut into their relief as if it had been a shot from the pistol he held in his hand. 'Will the magistrates believe I was simply defending my property when I shot you, Mellon?' he asked, gesturing for Tobias to back away from Mariah and stand against the wall. Brent rolled onto his back and lay still.

'I will have to wait for my servants to return with the carriage and then they will be viable witnesses.' He grinned maliciously at Mariah. 'Will they not?'

'What use are we to you dead?' she asked.

'I bow to your superior understanding, Miss Fox. You will of course be of no use to me dead, but you were of far more use to me when Mellon did not know your whereabouts than you are now that he has discovered you alive and inviolate.'

Tobias jumped forward, but Wellwood pointed the pistol at Mariah's head and he stilled. Brent opened one eye and groaned in pain.

'I see you have not completely lost your military training and skills, Mellon. Pity you did not put them into action before you came blundering in here. It would have suited us both better if Miss Fox had been able to visit my country estate for a day or two. Now we are left with a multitude of problems that were unforeseen when it was Lady Daisy who might have been my guest.'

John Brent tried to rise, but could not, and had to content himself with a murderous oath. Tobias saw how Wellwood assessed the way his friend moved and began to realise they had underrated the nature of this evil man. He was well prepared for the darker deeds necessary to kidnap young females, and would not be easy to defeat. Where were Linklater and Goreton?

'Do not do anything heroic and ultimately stupid, Brent. Had you swallowed your infernal pride a year ago and offered for the chit on the terms she described to Amarinta, she would not be a target for those of us who have neither reputation nor fortune . . . '

'Nor conscience, pride, or honour,' Mariah interjected forcefully.

Wellwood shifted his weight and kicked Brent hard on his body. He kept the pistol trained on Mariah and curled his lip in a sneer when she stifled a scream.

'You see, Miss Fox, all women are unable to control their tongues, and must expect consequences of their thoughtless words. While I do hope to hear more of your homilies on good breeding, perhaps Mr Brent would prefer you to keep quiet.'

Tobias seethed. He had never felt so powerless.

'I may not take you to task as I did my sister,' Wellwood continued, 'only because I have to maintain this distance between us. Once my servants return and these men are restrained, then we must see whether you bruise as easily as she.'

Black murder seized Tobias's brain.

★ ★ ★

Mariah swallowed hard. She had spoken out without fear for herself, but also without thought of the consequences, and now Mr Brent was in greater pain because of her actions.

Peter Sharp had said she had no appreciation of consequences, and this afternoon Tobias had agreed with him, but it was the sickening thud as Wellwood's riding boot met John Brent's ribs that made her understand how she erred. Intelligence alone was not enough to live by, she realised. A person needed common sense as well.

There was a commotion in the hallway behind Wellwood, but he did not turn toward it. The pistol pointed at her remained straight in his steady hand. Mariah would not allow herself to despair. Where was Tilly? Tobias had said she was fainting but alive. Would she alert the watch when she regained her senses? Wellwood's voice cut across her thoughts.

'Do not try any heroics, Mellon. My servants are unrefined men. You will not want to provoke their attention to yourself or your lady.'

'What do you want to gain from this, Wellwood? Several people know we are here, and your idea that you might shoot us as trespassers will not defend you before the law. You have been seen too often in our company to claim you did not recognise us,' Tobias said from behind her. She could not see him, but his voice was calm and she drew strength from it.

'I need money, Mellon. I have debts and I have promised these men a large pay-off for assisting in Lady Daisy's visit to my estate. A visit you and Miss Fox have prevented. I need twenty thousand pounds in cash and I need security for the future. It will suit me to have your acres of woodland copses assigned to me.' Wellwood nudged Brent with the toe of his boot. 'And you, sirra, can assign your newly discovered coalfield to me. These assignations will be deemed to be gambling debts.'

Mariah was horrified. Her precipitate action in coming here to find Amarinta — and she had not yet located that young person — was the cause of this. But worse, she feared, was to come.

'Should you need further persuasion, Mellon, you may watch as the lady's favours are enjoyed by my men. There are four of them . . . '

*   *   *

Heavy footsteps resounded through the house and Mariah's eyes were drawn to the men pushing into the room. Surprisingly, they were dressed to fit into the highest level of society. Was this another example of how they had misjudged Wellwood's cunning? Did he employ sprigs of the upper echelons fallen on hard times to do his brutish work?

'There *were* four of them,' the first man said calmly as Mariah's eyes widened in surprise. He sprang across the floor behind Wellwood and brought a short, thick branch down on the outstretched wrist holding that pistol. She leapt off the chair as it discharged into the floor at her feet.

Tobias gathered her into his arms and hauled her out of the way. The two newcomers kept up their assault on Wellwood. Suddenly the first man yelped with pain. He dropped to his knees and Mariah saw blood spurting from a wound in his upper arm. Rolling out of the action, he gripped his arm, but still the blood spurted, soaking his clothes.

'Linklater!' Tobias shouted. 'Goreton, he's got a knife!' Tobias thrust her farther into the corner and leapt toward the rolling bundle of men on the floor.

Mariah could not watch the fight and turned instead to the injured. Seeing John Brent had managed to rise as far as his knees and was crawling across to his friend, Mariah stooped and lifting the skirt of her dress, tugged hard on the petticoat beneath. She felt it tear and give sufficiently to let her step out of it. Moving along the wall and behind the chair she'd been held in, she reached Brent.

'Lean on me, Mr Brent,' she said, and assisted him into a sitting position. 'It may be best if you do not move at present.' She hoped he would follow her advice, but could do no more. It was the man Tobias had called Linklater who concerned her the most.

She caught the material of her ruined petticoat between her teeth and tore a strip from the cotton. Working as quickly as she could, she wound it around the man's upper arm and pulled tightly. He groaned and she cast a worried glance at his bleached face. Was she too late? The bleeding continued despite her efforts.

She crawled to the fireplace, narrowly avoiding a flying boot, and tipped over the kettle of spills and kindling kept there. Selecting a thin piece of kindling, she half-crawled, half-shuffled back to Linklater, and inserted the stick into her bandage, trapping it. The bleeding slowed. When it threatened to speed up again, she turned the stick a little. The bleeding stopped.

'Mariah,' Tobias said with a catch in his voice, and she looked up to see her earl with his clothes dishevelled and torn, and blood across his face. She started with fright but did not release her hold on the makeshift tourniquet.

'It is his blood,' Tobias said, nodding toward the prone shape of Wellwood stretched across the floor.

'Miss Fox,' the man who must be Goreton said, 'let me take over from you, ma'am. I was a surgeon in Mellon's regiment.' He was breathing hard, and he too had been injured. Red scars were lifting across his chin and Mariah suspected his nose was broken.

Brent still did not move from his sitting position, and Mariah's spirits sank lower than she could have believed. All these people, and Tilly — wherever she was — had been injured because she had not thought through the consequences of her actions. Why would Tobias wish to marry her now? She must release him from their betrothal at the earliest opportunity.

15

Mariah sat in the morning room two weeks later and fiddled with the essay on her lap. She watched her papa moving from his desk at the back of the big room toward the open doors into the garden, and smiled. The doctor's advice had resulted in much change in her father's condition. He was eating regular meals and drinking a lot of water drawn from a particular well which was known to be clean and clear. Josh went with him on walks around the streets, and recently they had been to Hyde Park in Tobias's carriage.

He will miss that when I break off my engagement, she thought. *We will all miss Josh, with his pleasant manner and quick intelligence, although I hope he will be allowed to return to us for further instruction in reading and writing.*

She had seen Tobias and Daisy several times since the day in Ogle Road when so many things had happened. She knew that the men Wellwood hired had been first restrained by Linklater and Goreton, and then released by local ne'er-do-wells while the fight raged. They had not been seen again. There was little chance of discovering their whereabouts in the warren of streets and courts surrounding London's fashionable areas.

Wellwood was dead. He had sustained a massive thrust during the fight that penetrated below his ribs and ruptured his spleen. Tobias and Goreton did not know which of them was responsible, but there had been a few anxious days while the authorities asked questions. Tobias's reputation, already damaged by his brother's death, was a stumbling block to the immediate acceptance of their version of events.

In the end, Amarinta, Wellwood's heir and new wife of Mr Reginald Barlow, came forward with her husband's permission, and spoke privately to the investigating magistrate. She brought with her a Mr Rodney Perkins who had been in service with her late mama, and whose testimony about the death of another member of the Wellwood staff, a second parlour-maid, was thought to be of interest.

The bell clanged in the hall and Josh answered the summons smartly. Within minutes he came into the room, followed by Tobias and Lady Mellon. Mariah received Constanzia's greetings diffidently. It would not be surprising if the lady wanted to berate her for putting her son and future son-in-law into such desperate danger.

'My dear Mariah,' Constanzia said, 'I cannot thank you enough for bringing all this dreadful business with the Wellwood family to an end.'

'Me?' Mariah asked, and caught sight of Tobias raising an eyebrow. She was no longer 'Miss Fox' to his mama, but 'Mariah'.

'Indeed. The maid, Tilly, has told our housekeeper how clever you were finding the place Sir Lucas lived, and how brave you were to attempt to rescue Amarinta. This is why she went to the magistrates, I am sure of it.'

'Does Tilly do well?' Mariah asked. She had not seen the girl for several days, and when she did, she was still shaky and tearful. Mariah had tried to cheer her by explaining how she had discovered the shard of glass set into the back of the chair she was held captive on. Further evidence, if any were needed, of how life had been lived in that household. It did not help. Tilly remained horrified by the way they had been manhandled, and scared that the magistrates would not believe Tobias and Goreton. Mariah was unable to reassure her, as she, too, was very concerned.

'She is much recovered since the magistrates announced there would be no charges,' the countess said with evident satisfaction. 'She insists on coming back to you in time to help with the wedding. I am glad we did not cancel it before. It showed the *ton* that his family were behind Tobias,' the countess concluded passionately.

'Mariah,' Tobias said, 'I hope you will forgive my neglect of you but I could not come while the investigations were ongoing. I believe Mama is right about Amarinta. Mr Barlow had a falling-out with his parent over the match, but it went ahead despite Lady Barlow's threat to cut them off during his minority.'

Mariah quailed at the thought that two more people had suffered as a result of her impetuous actions. She was amazed to see the countess draw herself up to her full four-feet-ten and turn a sceptical eye on her son.

'It is my belief that those young persons will waste no time in making the woman a grandmamma. She seems to me to be exactly the type of person who will succumb to such actions, and the scandal will be forgotten,' she said. 'Now, Mariah, where is your papa? I intend to have him escort me round

Hyde Park in the carriage.'

'He will miss your attentions, ma'am, once you set off on your trip to Spain,' Mariah said. 'He is in the garden.'

'I do not travel to Spain,' the countess said. Mariah feared to ask any questions as the lady's expression did not encourage them.

'I am sorry to hear that, your ladyship,' she said, and walked to the back windows with her visitor. *Was the countess staying in England because Tobias had said he would not marry her?* Mariah wondered. His mother had said, *'I am glad we did not cancel the wedding before.'* Did that mean he had come to ask to break it off now that a suitable decision had come from the authorities?

'Mariah.' Tobias spoke quietly. 'I have my curricle and I wish you to come driving with me, please,' he said, and his brown eyes, recently so full of sadness, were a little less severe.

* * *

Tobias drove skilfully through the late-morning traffic and was soon set on the road to Richmond. They travelled for several miles before he addressed her.

'We are to spend the night with John Brent and his sisters. They wish to meet you,' he said as if he had just told her they were taking a turn around some pleasure grounds.

'I have nothing with me, Tobias. No clothes, no necessities, no maid,' she protested.

'I know you miss Tilly's company, and I would have sent her back to you before this, but the housekeeper was adamant. She has released her from her care today, however, and you will find her at Richmond with all the things you think you need,' he said.

'Think I need!' Mariah protested. 'Since when did you become an expert on my needs?'

'I know I am not an expert, my love, but I try to learn.' He tooled the horses, and Mariah saw they had left the road and were pulling into the yard of an inn. The groom jumped down from behind, and Tobias assisted Mariah out of the vehicle.

'I have reserved a private parlour here. It is a little unconventional as we will not be married until Friday, but I wished to have a conversation with you that would not be interrupted by relatives or well-wishers,' he said, leading her into the building. The landlord bustled about, and very quickly they were settled in a small room with easy chairs, a sofa, and tables. A decanter of brandy and a jug of lemonade sat with some glasses and some small almond biscuits.

'Now, my beloved Mariah, tell me why you do not wish to marry me,' he said, and she was sure the twinkle that had attracted her attention to him when he rescued her from the mud of the yards was back in his eyes.

'How did you know? You are laughing at me,' she said accusingly, 'when it is very clear that I cannot marry you.

Look at the damage my headstrong behaviour caused. How can such a person make a worthy countess?'

'Damage?' Tobias asked, clearly amazed. He had known she was holding back, but not why. 'Do you fear that I blame you, or that John and Tilly blame you?'

'What about your friend Linklater, or Amarinta and Reginald Barlow?' she asked.

'And, of course, Goreton's wife. She is most displeased that his good looks are marred for life by his broken nose,' Tobias said, barely suppressing his laughter at her face of doom.

'You are laughing. Why do you find it funny?'

'Goreton, Linklater and I have been soldiers, my love. What do we think about a bang on the head or a broken nose, when we saw the sights we saw?'

'I concede they must have been worse,' Mariah agreed, 'but Wellwood was right. I did not think of the consequences, and he made Mr Brent suffer great pain when he was already injured,' she said, almost pleading for him to understand. It was so difficult to be here alone with him and to know she was about to lose such a right forever. 'I am a blue-stocking and unfit to be any kind of countess.'

Tobias stood up and moved across the room to sit beside her on the sofa. 'I swore to myself that I would not do this until I had heard you agree that the wedding would go ahead as planned,' he said, before he pulled her into his arms and kissed her.

Mariah felt his warm lips cover hers and his arms gather her to him as if she were so precious he could not envisage life without her. She squeezed her hand out of his embrace and caught the back of his head to hold him close. This was such wanton behaviour, but it would not happen again, and she needed to have some memories of him to savour when she was ensconced in Bath with Miss Venables.

He set her apart and gazed deeply

into her soul. Mariah felt the blush stain her cheeks and neck, and wondered if it were possible to blush all over.

'Mariah,' Tobias said, 'I started our association in the wrong way by laying hands on your person. I continued it by telling other people I wanted to make you my countess without consulting your wishes. I organised an assignation that meant your reputation was destroyed in the eyes of all the educationalists who might offer you employment and take your ideas seriously. For these failings I apologise and beg your forgiveness,' Tobias said.

'Why are you ignoring my feelings now, Tobias? Why are you setting aside my guilt without addressing the implications it must have for the position you wished me to fill?' she asked, but less forcefully than she had intended.

She was beginning to wonder if she could continue the engagement after all. Tobias was a difficult man to love. He had certain failings. He had just listed them and she was unable to argue with his case. He had behaved single-mindedly in pursuit of her. Did all young women like to be pursued single-mindedly? Perhaps she should consult Daisy on this point.

'We do not blame you, my love. The world is a better place without Lucas Wellwood, and you helped to force him into the open. I may wish you had confided certain information to me earlier, but I do not doubt you acted as you thought best,' he said.

'Why does your mama cancel her trip?' she asked.

'Because Daisy has accepted John Brent. It seems she had thought to take the chit abroad, and let John stew over her absence so that he would come round to living on Daisy's money. The discovery of coal, of course, meant he could ask her to marry him in the knowledge he could support her,' Tobias said quietly.

'So Lady Mellon was acting when she made so much fuss about wanting to live under the sun and speak Spanish every day?' Mariah's eyes filled with hope.

'She had us all fooled. Apparently no amount of sun compensates for the superior comforts the Mellon Dower House will provide when compared with a country so recently recovering from war.' Tobias grinned. 'Did you believe I had told Mama we would not be married, and she was back to hunting for a suitable wife for me?'

Mariah nodded. 'I did.'

'Did that not make you unhappy?' he asked, and his voice was tinged with hope.

'Yes, I was unhappy.'

Tobias slid from the sofa and knelt before her.

'Mariah, will you please agree to marry me on Friday, if I promise to arrange as many classes as the week can hold at all of my homes?'

She shook her head, and Tobias's eyes filled with shock.

'I will marry you on Friday, my love,

because I wish to be your wife and lifelong companion,' she said. 'And . . .'

Tobias did not wait to hear any more from his future wife, but kissed her until she struggled for breath, and then kissed her again.

And again.

THE END

TAKE ME, I'M YOURS

Gael Morrison

Melissa D'Angelo is tired of being the only twenty-four-year-old virgin in Seattle. Before entering medical school, she needs a lover with no strings attached. Harvard Law School graduate Jake Mallory loves women and they love him. But a pregnancy scare with a woman he barely knew birthed a vow of celibacy and a growing need for love, family and commitment. The moment Jake and Melissa meet at a local club, passion ignites. But Melissa can't allow sex to lead to love — and love and family are all Jake wants . . .

BABY ON LOAN

Liz Fielding

Jessie is temporarily caring for her adorable baby nephew when she gets evicted from her apartment! She has no choice but to let Patrick Dalton think she's a single mother, so that he'll let her stay with him. The last thing he wants is Jessie and her baby bringing chaos to his serene home — but in no time his life is filled with laughter and the very beautiful Jessie. Until he discovers that his growing love for his houseguests is based on a lie . . .

THE ANTIQUE LOVE

Helena Fairfax

Wyoming man Kurt Bold is looking for a wife, and he's determined his choice will be based on logic. Penny Rosas is the lively and romantic owner of an antique shop in London. When Kurt hires Penny to refurbish his Victorian town house, he treats her like he would his kid sister. But it's not long before the logical heart Kurt guards so carefully is opening up to new emotions, in a most disturbing way . . .

PRUDENCE AND THE MIGHTY FLYNN

Sarah Evans

Dumped a week before her wedding on account of being 'boring', Prudence Stark decides to turn her humdrum world upside down and live adventurously — trying all the things she's always been too shy, too sensible or too chicken to do. She leaves her teaching job in England to fly to the great Australian outback, where she meets gorgeous cattle station owner — and commitment-phobe — Flynn Maguire. Though the chemistry between them is hot, Flynn finds Pru's new outrageous take on life unsettling — while she's intent only on having fun . . .